Even The Ants Have Names

*Anthology of Short Stories
by new women writers*

Guest Editor Gerry Wardle

First published Autumn 2002 by:
Diamond Twig
5 Bentinck Road
Newcastle upon Tyne
NE4 6UT
Tel/Fax 0191 273 5326
Email: diamond.twig@virgin.net
www.diamondtwig.co.uk

Typeset in Palatino

Printed by Peterson Printers, Jarrow

Reprinted 2007

ISBN 0 9539196 33
ISBN 978-0-9539196-3-5

Diamond Twig acknowledges the
financial assistance of Northern Arts

Contents

Ride

by Linda Leatherbarrow

If you take the tube to Victoria, longing to be out of this hazy city, to be on your own, where each step is a miracle of moving forward with no side-stepping or going round, the line of your thoughts staying in line with your feet; if you trek up the escalator, adjust your backpack for the fourth time, take a swig from your water bottle, then pass through the shiny new shopping mall, smelling of melting chocolate, go out at the back and cross Buckingham Palace Road, smelling of fried sunlight, you will come to Victoria Coach Station and, if you slog through Departures, dodging bodies draped across the floor, sleeping or otherwise, trying not to tread on feet, hands, suitcases, pigeons, or empty crisp packets, you will come to Bay 19 where, because you are forty minutes early, being the sort of person who cannot stand being late, you will find yourself in a privileged position, sitting on the front seat of the Glasgow coach, to the left of the driver and behind the big front window, where you can stretch your legs and nibble peanut butter and cucumber sandwiches, Battenberg cake, hard boiled eggs and tangerines, thoughtfully provided for you by Mum, who obviously has no sense of smell and worries that you would have tried to last out the journey solely on a packet of chewing gum (and she'd be right; just the thought of a hard boiled egg makes you heave), and where you can stare straight ahead at the road, at unimpeded vistas of landscapes to come, savage yellow rectangles of oil seed rape, the smear of cities tucked into distant folds, and, closer up, splattered bugs on your window and an Uncle Bulgaria womble swinging by its scarf from the central mirror like a felon from a gibbet, making you think of death and, because there is really no point in thinking about

4

death (it's not going to change anything, is it?) and because death is pretty much the same as divorce, Dad going off to Birmingham to live with his boyfriend and stepping right off the planet, or might just as well have for all you've seen of him, and because you don't want to be thinking about this (again), you consider digging out of your anorak pocket your second-hand leather bound volume of Heidegger but it seems pretentious, risky even, and you wish you'd brought Hannibal or even Man and Boy by Tony Parsons which someone at work recommended last week, though you hate Tony Parsons and think he's a jerk, only watching him on The Late Show because it's important to keep up so you've got something to talk about at work (you have a Saturday job at Dixons, Wood Green) and, because you're slightly in love with Tom Paulin (you're always slightly in love with older men, especially those with Irish brogues and thinning hair who know far more than you will ever know - knowledge being like slate grey lentils bought from a Turkish grocer's, trickling through your fingers until only the gravel bits are left behind), you decide to talk to the driver though there is a notice, right in front of you, saying Do Not Talk To The Driver, but you do anyway and discover his name is Marty, that he plays trumpet for the Salvation Army, lives in Southampton and has already been driving all night and this is overtime (not strictly allowed) and you tell him that your name is Mira Rainbird, that you're doing an extra year at school in order to re-take your A Levels, are going to walk the entire West Highland Way by yourself, and that you, that is Mum, owns a West Highland terrier called Steed - after Steed in The Avengers - then, when you're halfway up the motorway, Marty pulls over into the slow lane, clicks on his microphone to address all the passengers, not just you, and asks that they join with him in thanking Their Maker that they have not yet arrived at the Pearly Gates, are not yet asking St. Peter's permission to pass through, unlike that lot in the other coach who passed through earlier, remember? (how could you forget when you and Marty had a full-on view?) that lot who skidded on an oil patch, smashed into the central barricade, zigzagged then mounted the bank, rolled down the other side into a reservoir and drowned, all of them, including the driver (Marty knows that this is what happened after they disappeared over the bank because Control have been onto him on the radio, checking if he got clear or is stuck in tailback) and, by now, you're thinking about bits of bodies, two fingers picked up in a glove, people wrapped in weed, down in the mud where they sink deeper and deeper until their flesh becomes mud, their bones piled hugger-mugger like the bones of all those people at Vesuvius, and you're wondering why people would choose to live on the skirts of a volcano, thinking about a programme on BBC Knowledge that you sat up watching late last night, with Mum, when you should have been going to bed early so as to be fresh for the journey, a programme called The Boiling Seas, which took nearly an hour to get to the boiling part and was mostly to do with carbon dioxide being taken up by the Amazon rain forest and stored, and it's possible you fell asleep because, apart from the title shot of flames licking waves, you can't remember any boiling, and now Marty is asking that we thank God for saving us from the fate that befell the three young soldiers, remember? (this you didn't see, passing by shortly after it happened) three young soldiers who were crushed in the back of their jeep by a Sainsbury's lorry, its driver falling asleep at the wheel just before Rugby, and here you can't help wondering (again) if it was entirely prudent of Marty to have used up all his legal driving miles last night and how much sleep deprivation is endemic among long distance drivers and, meanwhile, Marty is explaining that he is a first-timer, straight out of training school, who has never before driven a coach all the way up the M6 from London to Glasgow, and that there should be a co-driver, to keep him company and take a turn at the wheel, only he called in sick and it's illegal for him (Marty) to drive for more than four hours without a comfort break but what can you do in these circumstances and so far so good, eh folks? and there is a ragged cheer of acknowledgment then one of the passengers - Robby from Swansea - comes down the gangway to ask if he can take the microphone to say something on behalf of his fellow passengers and Marty says it's irregular but, sure, why not? and you think this is so embarrassing and cringe back into your seat and wish, momentarily, that you were not at the front, out in the open, where Robbie, who has something wrong with his nose which makes it look as if a war has been fought over every pore, and something wrong with his genitals which roll inside his trousers like a rugger ball, sprays you with saliva as he adds his, and everybody else's thanks, to those expressed before, remarking that in spite of not being able to take a comfort break on this epic, and he does mean epic, journey, Marty has driven like a hero, and he does mean hero, and he has no doubt that we will, eventually, reach Glasgow, in spite of delays, tailback, thunderstorms, floods, thirty-two miles of traffic cones near Watford, the fallen bridge at Coventry, and he talks on, listing and spewing like a drunken missionary, clutching the microphone, swaying with the motion of the coach, now doing eighty-eight miles per hour (you can see the Speedo), gabbling on in spite of the notice which says Strictly No Standing Beside The Driver until, blushing, he wipes his forehead with a white cotton handkerchief with an R embroidered in one corner, and retires to his seat in a volley of claps and cheers and a feeble rendition of For He's A Jolly Good Fellow, started up by Monica at the back, whose enormous chest is falling out of her scoop-neck shocking pink T-shirt emblazoned with the legend Eyes-Off-Dick-Head, who now comes forward to offer Marty a little something from her hip flask, just to keep you going, darling, everyone needs a little something to keep them going, in spite of the notice saying It Is An Offence To Consume Alcohol On This Vehicle, and Marty, having said earlier that anyone found drinking will be forcibly removed, who now says he doesn't mind if he does, and so do you, and soon there is a party going on - and you're more relieved than you can say that you kept the Heidegger in your pocket and didn't let on for an moment that you are the sort who reads - a party just at the front, you understand, because, at the back, some passengers are trying to sleep and someone's baby is almost murdered by a medical student who is revising for his exams (which he has to sit tomorrow), and you are secretly in sympathy with him because you think, if you ever had a baby yourself, and you're sure you wouldn't but, if you ever did, you'd be the sort who would shake it and kill it and have to stand trial for homicide or babycide, or whatever, and you imagine the baby's coffin, immaculate with heaped up white lilies with fat orange stamens dripping brick-red pollen over the sides, until it's stained and streaked like a tiger coffin - a tiger cub coffin - and, while you're imagining it going down, past the plastic grass, into the worm-wriggling earth, the mother wallops the student with a Nike sports bag containing thirty-six disposable nappies, thirty of which are still clean, two packets of Baby Wipes, four full bottles of formula milk and two empty ones, six brand new Babygros and a silver foil twist of black ganja which the man in her health food store promised is the very best, a coming home present for her boyfriend - if the baby will only just go to sleep and stay alive

8

and keep breathing, if he (the student) will keep his filthy mitts to himself and stop eyeing her up and shouting at the baby, who is only crying after all, which is what babies do, isn't it? and what does he think she can do about it, stuck on the coach like this without a break? and now there is a bit of a riot with five or six of the passengers coming forward to say Stop The Coach, and Marty saying that he's Only Doing His Job and he can't let them off, even if we are stationary, and to use the chemical toilet at the rear, and someone shouting that that's not a chemical toilet but a cesspit and a health hazard and if Marty doesn't stop the coach this instant he will open the Emergency Door because there is someone here who is seriously travel sick and is going to throw up, correction has thrown up, so LET US OFF but Marty grinds into gear again, lurches forward, and you wonder if he's planning to go up the backside of the car transporter in front, or over the mini with the little kiddies inside, sticking their fingers up at him and blowing raspberries? and, at this point, you realize just how much you're enjoying yourself and wish you could be on this coach forever, the air rich with blasphemy and swearing, the clear promise of violence, the smell of Marty's sweat, ripe as the smell of the hard boiled egg which, somehow, you're eating because it's getting dark and you're beginning to think about morning and how far away it is and whether, when you're this far north, past Wigan, it stays lighter at night and there might be an aurora borealis, like in Local Hero when Burt Lancaster tells his anger therapist to fuck off and flies from his Global Headquarters in Houston, Texas, to the northerly tip of Scotland because he's obsessed with comets and all things astronomical, where you can see every star because the air is so clean, the light so pellucid, where you're going (if you ever get off this coach), and you keep looking straight ahead through your big front window because it is yours now, only yours and Marty's, the others having given up and gone back, sulking and smoking in spite of the notice saying No Smoking, and you're beginning to worry about passive smoking and Marty says it's a shame about the air conditioning, he doesn't know why they build these coaches with windows that can't be opened, a shame, on his first trip and all, it's enough to put you off, and he should have stuck it out at his last job which turns out to have been guarding offenders in Brixton nick, and you begin to wonder about the word offender and who is offended and why, until you're almost on the point of digging out the Heidegger seeing that, now it's dark, no one will notice you reading and, anyway, half of them are asleep, when you notice how beautiful it's getting, tail lights up ahead spilling over the hills, streams of lights flying up, streams of lights falling down, and all the things you can't see are simply blacker parts of the night and you're riding, in this great illuminated vehicle, like an exile riding into a country you thought you'd never see again, because, although you haven't been to Scotland, your mother was born there; it's in the blood and London is just the place you live, or rather, instead of an exile, you're a ghost who's forgotten who they were but pines to be back, until, after all, none of this matters because you're too busy soaking up the atmosphere of concentration, duty and responsibility, bravely borne by Marty, and it's as if you and Marty are one and it's up to you to deliver the passengers safely to their destination, passengers who are melding and sinking together in the treacle blackness, mouths open, arms loose, the coach warm with the breath of their sleeping; even the mother of the almost murdered baby is sleeping, her baby sleeping in the nest of her arms, and, on the seat beside them, the medical student, also sleeping, dreams of attending a dissection in St. Bartholomew's Hospital, the body on the table recently dug up from its grave and carried into the hospital in a laundry basket (he will write about this in his exam tomorrow and lose marks for digression), while, on the fourth row from the back, Robbie from Swansea, neither dreaming nor sleeping, stares out of his side window at the flicking trace-lines of hedges, branches leafed with rooks waiting for daybreak and thermals that will rise from the morning tarmac, and thinks that it has been a good journey, in spite of everything, and that he has distinguished himself, yes he means distinguished, in coming forward to speak up for them all, in being the kind of person who seizes the moment and talks into microphones, and thinks that, tomorrow, he will ask for promotion and, even if he doesn't get it, it will be enough to know that he asked, and, on the seat behind his, Monica sleeps with her mouth open, her generous chest rising and falling like an ocean becalmed, while you sit back on the front seat, entirely awake, having eaten the peanut butter sandwiches and given some of your Battenberg to Marty, (thanks very much, don't mind if I do) and wonder if, on the way back, you might hop off at Birmingham because there is nothing to stop you calling in on Dad and, anyway, it might be preferable to catch him on his patch rather than wait forever for him to haul himself down to London where he could bump into Mum, then you peel a tangerine, watch the lights of faraway places and a silver quarter moon skipping from left to right of the coach then back again, the road bending while appearing to be straight, and think this is grand, this being away from home, this being on your own for the first time, truly on your own.

The Student

by Linda Leatherbarrow

Christopher has a special dispensation for being late, his tutor having accepted that this condition is better not pried into and might, if left unchallenged, gradually disappear. Christopher hates being late. He flies in, scarf ends flapping, coat falling off his shoulders, 'Sorry, so very sorry, thank you...' hoping, as he sinks into a seat, that his fellow students will imagine him running from the station then up the stairs. It takes him a further half hour to settle and, until he does, he can't make sense of what anyone says. Smiling, he leans forward as if paying close attention. This tutor is better than previous ones. The last one was at him as soon as he came through the door. If she'd had x-ray eyes she would have seen him hovering on the other side, his hand reaching for the handle then falling back again.

Today he follows a new strategy - leave early, walk around the vicinity, allow himself to be distracted. He jumps off the tube a stop before his usual one, cuts through Russell Square and across the road. Up ahead a clump of tweedy women climb out of a coach and block the pavement - dry cleaning, dry sherry, Chanel No 5. Individually they're probably charming but collectively they bring to mind all those times he's been button-holed at parties. 'And what do you do in Life, Christopher?'

It's years since he did anything in Life. Once he worked in the office of his uncle's factory on the Great West Road, a factory turning out fancy silver furniture for wedding cakes. Once, though he finds this hard to believe now, he played lead guitar with a band. After that, there were shops, forecourts, pubs, a stint putting spectacle frames together and then...well, it's hard to remember, hard to figure out. Life is not something he wants to consider, not now when he's trying to get himself to class on time.

He brushes long black hair away from his face, squeezes his scarf tighter round his throat, and strides past high railings. This is better. He used to come here from school. Saint Francis Catholic School for Boys was very keen on this place. Every year, they shunted their boys through its corridors, a treat Christopher looked forward to - the mummies, the rock crystal skull, ferocious magic on casual display. He hurries in; there is still at least an hour to kill.

But where there used to be a shabby closed off courtyard with the dome of the old Reading Room in its centre, he finds a huge glazed-over space, the Reading Room newly encased in a sparkling white marble skin. Twin flights of stairs winding round it. You can almost hear the harps, not to mention a celestial choir in full voice, but Christopher, who is no longer religious, imagines a roof garden with a fountain. Maybe he's been watching too many gardening programmes. He can't resist gardening programmes, loves them. Only yesterday he bought himself a bunch of scarlet silk poppies from a Pound Shop, compensation for the slush and draggle of December.

Setting off up the right hand flight, he runs his hands over the chamfered edges, lets his fingertips trail along the groove in the parapet until they're coated with white dust. He can't help stopping to stare at the stretch of glass above his head, warm cobalt at the edge, coolest ultramarine in the middle. At the top, there's a barricade - Restaurant Closed - but just as he's turning away, he spots a side passage and a door.

'Allow me.'

Flashes of gold light fly off the flat planes of the stranger's spectacles.

'Thank you,' says Christopher, seeing the crowd in the

room ahead, thinking that this is not at all where he wants to be. 'Thank you.'

It's darker inside the room, like shade under trees. Edging in, he begins to circulate. Imagine going up an escalator and suddenly noticing that, on the opposite escalator, every second or third person is someone you recognize. You don't know what to say. 'Hi,' you start. 'Hello.' Then peter out. There's the little Egyptian with lapis lazuli eyes who looks as if she's just stepped out of a space ship, Chairman Mao with his right hand raised in salute, the discus thrower, (well they would have him, wouldn't they?) a seated Buddha, and Tara with her elongated ears, high round breasts, narrow waist. What's so odd is finding them together. Usually they're segregated - Romans in the Roman gallery, Greeks in the Greek, and so on, never higgledy-piggledy like this.

One at a time, thinks Christopher. You're asked to have a group conversation but you have to introduce yourself first. That's how it is with groups - names first. At least that's how they do it at the City Lit. The ice breaker. Go round one at a time. 'How are you? Good to see you again.' Then go round and ask, 'How does it feel to be here together? Working collectively for the first time? Because I'm assuming this is a first for you. For me. You're used to being in groups but you haven't been in this group before, have you?'

Although geography and chronology have been disposed of, categories haven't. Somehow Christopher isn't surprised. Abstraction. Drapery. Guardians. He doesn't know where to start. Others? A little to the left of Venus, is the big Nigerian, the one with black and white markings, filed teeth and raised facial scarring, his favourite Nigerian, but now he sees there's something uncomfortable in the way the hands are held out, palms up; the eyes are impassive but the hands say sorry.

'You wear your heart on your sleeve,' said his lover. 'It puts people off.'

'I'm not talking about people,' he said. 'I'm talking about you!'

And there he is slamming his fist at the wall, making a hole when he only wanted a gesture, a ragged black hole in a wall that turns out to be plasterboard.

'Jesus!' she said. 'That is it. Oh, Jesus Christ!'

'It's only a wall,' he said. 'What does it matter?'

There he is kneeling on the floor, crying and spreading Polyfilla, watching the grey sludge turn slowly white. It's rough and lumpy, needs sanding, but at least it's filled again, the hole hidden.

'You might say sorry,' she said, just before she left.

Now he lowers himself onto a bench, wedges his bag between his feet. There is an eight line poem in the bag, iambic, trochaic, seventeen copies, one for the tutor, one for himself, fifteen for the other students. His heart hammers. He will have to go in a moment. He's too hot, a slow burn in his head, top lip sweaty, inside of his elbows, backs of his knees.

The worst thing is knowing, with absolute certainty, no two ways about it, that the homework which he has laboured over all week, is worthless trite rubbish, pretentious nonsense. What was he thinking about? In half an hour he will have to hit the streets and by then it will be dark. The other students will be pouring towards the college, would-be actors, computer programmers, those wishing to manage their anger, reach their inner child or touch their toes. He will have to squeeze through them all. He will have to get there on time. It's hopeless. He might as well go home now.

Except he can't. No matter how difficult it is, he must go to his class. He's firm on that. Only by going, can it get any easier and can he turn things round. It's too late for Life but personal satisfaction, artistic achievement, those are still on the agenda. He has to believe that but, meanwhile, here he is in a room full of ethnographic plunder with the lights dimmed. If he could just remember some of the other students' names. There's a woman he likes - they went for a drink together - but he can't remember her name. It's ridiculous. After eight weeks he still can't remember her name.

Slumped on the bench, he listens to the controlled thud of the doors as newcomers file in and out. There are two doors, one on either side of the room and he sits between them. He doesn't want to be here, not with all these people tip-toeing over the carpet. Are they all killing time? They remind him of the heron on Finsbury Park lake, on the look-out but too well fed to care. People with bags and mobile phones, people on their own, in pairs, a young girl in a tinsel crown and a lavender fleece, school kids, tourists, the bored and the amazed. Why are they whispering? As if any of these guys would mind - the dead shaman prepared for burial, the Hindu goddess without her head.

Do not touch. Even the lightest touch damages the exhibits. But looking isn't enough. Never mind the implied expectation that it is, or should be, that the sculptor or the subject is somehow staring out of blank eye sockets, that you have only to look hard enough to communicate. Who's to stop him and what real harm would it do? Christopher has a dim memory of being shouted at once before. 'Hands off, laddie!' But there's only one warden, half asleep at the far end of the room. Keeping his face blank, Christopher stands up, strolls past the tattooed woman with her protuberant stomach, past a Rain Giver from Jamaica, past the big Nigerian again. Adrenaline rushes round his body. Inside his jacket pockets, his hands are prickling. Which one? He goes round twice before he comes to a decision.

Prince Khaemwaset is carved out of ordinary sandstone conglomerate. He's Egyptian, over three thousand years old and beginning to crumble, his polished surface interrupted, his chest cracked open, revealing water worn pebbles, fragments of pre-existing rocks bonded in alluvial cement.

The pragmatic Christopher says, 'This is crazy. What can possibly happen?' The superstitious Christopher tells him to stand back. Stand well back. He steps closer, stretches out his hand. His hand trembles. What does he expect - a twist of stellar energy? To be burnt, or frozen? Will Prince Khaemwaset speak to him in a spectral voice? The End Of The World Is Nigh, nuclear dark descends tomorrow, asteroids, insect plagues, cloned zombies, the curse of the Mummy's Tomb, I am the God of Hell-fire! But it's just as he thought. He touches Prince Khaemwaset's innards and no lightning comes to strike him down; there is no voice, only a calm emptiness he takes as a gift.

When he slips into the classroom, he's forty minutes late, the tutor has given her usual talk and the room is brighter than usual.

'Now,' says the tutor, 'homework. Did everyone do the exercise?'

Christopher smiles and leans forward.

She begins to go round the class, each student handing out their copies then reading their work aloud, in turn.

'Christopher?' she says.

He takes a single piece of paper from his bag, coughs.

'Sorry, no copies.' Coughs again. 'My chest...'

'Take your time,' says the tutor.

He gives a final cough, pats his chest, clears his throat, then reads aloud.

'Carved in air...,' he begins.

The poem is not iambic, not trochaic. It has no rhymes and

the syntax is a mess. Listening to himself read, he thinks it's not even a poem. It's about finding yourself alone and not knowing any more how to be with people, not knowing if you can trust them, not knowing who you are, when everything you say or think, everything you feel, is wrong. It's about making yourself solid again.

Stupid, thinks Christopher, reading on. Why didn't you go with the original? I haven't done what I was meant to, they'll either laugh at me or ignore me. But when he finishes, they clap. They don't usually clap. In fact he can't remember them clapping before and the woman he likes is smiling at him.

He's almost certainly blushing. He watches them talking about his poem but can't hear them, back in that time when all he did was cry, when anything could set him off, a hungry child on tv, two words left off a postcard - a bare signature instead of 'love from...'

He sits there thinking that enough time has passed to put half a self together, that half a self is better than no self and not to be sniffed at. They're looking at him, smiling.

'Would anyone like to go for a drink?' he blurts.

'I would,' says the tutor. 'After class.'

He drinks bitter shandy with Bella-Marie.

The others are there too but he's squeezed up in a corner with Bella-Marie, the woman he likes, and all he can think about is the way her tongue comes out and licks stray froth off her upper lip, the way her hair slithers over her eyes. She's wearing leggings under her skirt because she's been to Dance Impro first. He tells her about the white dome and Prince Kaemwaset.

'Did you know,' she says,' (his heart sinks at this; it always sinks when anyone says this, dive-bombs to the permafrost floor) 'Did you know that conglomerate was high status stone, difficult to work with, therefore extra prestigious?'

It turns out she took Kingship and Religion in Ancient Egypt last year and Hieroglyphs the year before. Christopher hauls himself back up to the light. It's good, isn't it, that they share an interest?

Later, he escorts her to Holborn tube then walks on to Liverpool Road, where he lives. Some of the street lights are missing and you can see the stars. He can't remember the names of the constellations and he's standing staring up at one that could be The Plough but might be Orion when he's jostled against a wall. A man goes through his pockets, takes his wallet. Christopher is sure that The Plough has seven stars. The hands go through his pockets while he counts.

'Give me your bag,' says the man.

'Why should I?' says Christopher.

'Because I've got a knife,' says the man.

After he's gone, Christopher can't remember what he looked like, only that he wore a baseball hat. He's a little annoyed about his bag and his wallet but he isn't frightened. Maybe he will be later. The main thing is he still has this afternoon's poem, in his head. He recites it to the drunks and stray dogs, to the rough sleepers, to anyone who passes, to the empty street, his front door, the fading glow-stars on the ceiling above his bed.

Even The Ants Have Names
by Mary Lowe

Eva crouches behind the sofa in the front room, willing her limbs to concertina into the tiny space next to the wall. The shimmying of slippers on carpet and the cool drone of voices is enough to make her want to disappear. She stays because she wants to know what's in her mother's head. She's been crouched there for too long and her legs have gone dead but one false move and the grown-ups will realise that she's hiding and there will be hell on. She can see the tweedy knee of Miss Dunbar Naismith angled like a jackknife under the chair. She hears the low throb of her mother's voice who asks about the people in the church and whether she has to wear a hat.

'The church welcomes anybody, particularly those who are… needy,' comes the squeaky voice of Miss Naismith. 'The dress code is entirely up to you.'

'I'm very pleased to hear that,' says her mother,' I've been praying now for so long. Myself and Eva, we struggle.' Her mother's voice drops to an almost inaudible level, 'To be honest, I've had all sorts of problems with her. Last week she threw someone's bag through a window at school and smashed a pane of glass which I had to pay for. She looks as quiet as a mouse but underneath… And her father is… her father works away a lot.'

Eva burns like hot glass. She pictures the plaintive face of her mother, her appealing eyebrows bent into a curl, the wrinkle in the forhead that forks her face in two. Her mother has a bellyful of problems and Eva is the worst of them. She's heard her mother praying at night with her hands clasped in front of her chest like a child. 'Dear Lord take Eva away and give her the strength to be good.' She'd heard her mother wailing in the middle of the night. But now she has the church. Her mother will go to church tomorrow. She goes most days to save her soul before it's too late. 'I have a soul as shadowy as a smokestack,' she says, 'and I need to make it clean'.

There are more cups of tea. They talk about Laburnam bushes and how fat the snails are this year. And eventually just as Eva is thinking that she'll never be able to move again,

Miss Naismith says she is off to see her next customer and the tweed skirt rides past. For a moment, Eva looks up into the frowning eyes of Miss Naismith and notices that she is brandishing a rolled up newspaper that she clutches like a truncheon.

Up in her bedroom, the windows are steamy. Outside she can see the green of the garden, the top of the fence, flowers in clumps of pink and orange and Mr Cox, the man-next-door as he trundles his wheelbarrow up and down. She writes 'Eva' on the window in big bold writing, then she tries it in joined up. 'Eva' she writes, as grown-up as anything. Then she copies the signature of Elizabeth the First and adds a mess of macramé underneath.

Eva R.

She is in the garden, muffled up. It's cold and the trees are waving. Mr Cox is on the other side of the fence, Maurice the cat is sitting by the silver birch and Mum is in the kitchen. Eva is counting the ants, swarming between the rockery and the Yukka. Some of the ants have names, the larger ones carrying a piece of twig or a stone, these she calls the beefy ones. She calls them Bert or Fred or David. Businesslike names. Boys names.

'Hey David, get one of your pals to help you,' she whispers. David takes no notice and carries on, oblivious. She stands up and brushes the dirt from her trousers. These are new trousers and Mum calls them slacks.

Mr Cox is nearly six foot two, sixtyish and wears a hat. Eva is seven and proud of it. Mr Cox is stiff-backed and speaks only sometimes. Eva likes that. She likes the way he says Good Morning and Good Afternoon to her and sometimes raises his hat is if she were a grown-up and he had to mind his manners.

The ants are counted, the pictures chalked along the

flagstones and the washing line pushed backwards and forwards to aid the drying of the washing. It is hard work; she is ready for a rest. Along the top of the fence on the other side she sees a hat moving backwards and forwards. She hears the sound of humming.

Eva wants to catch his attention so she picks up a stone.

'Hello Mr Cox,' the stone says. 'This is me, Eva. What a lovely day we're having.'

She throws the stone in the air. Up it goes and lands with a thin crash on her side of the fence. The hat continues to move backwards and forwards. She picks another stone, a slightly larger one. This stone says something similar to the first, only in a louder voice. She clutches it tightly, pulls back her shoulder blade and throws it as hard as she can. The stone skims the top of the fence and lands with a soft plop on the other side.

Eva creeps up to the fence, below the place where the stone has landed and waits for 'Afternoon Eva. How are you today?' But there is no sound except for a faint rustle of clothing and the thud of a spade as it hits the earth.

One last go. A stone the size of a tea plate. A piece of flint; chalky on one side and glinty on the other. A real shouty stone. Mr Cox would like this one. She rubs spit on the black side and turns it in the sun. Two hands this time. She holds the thing in the sling of her hands and heaves upwards.

The stone is shouting. Mr Cox is shouting. Eva hides below the rim of the fence.

'What the...?' she hears.

She runs. Through the kitchen, her feet skidding on lino 'What the hell do you think you're doing?' shrieks Mum. Too late. She is up the stairs, into the bedroom. Carpet, bed, eiderdown. She pulls the covers tightly around her, breathing thick foxy breaths as she waits for the sound of the door.

In the film of the Turkish muscle men, a giant column of flesh emerges from the lacy steam and crushes a cockroach between his fingers. There is a crack and a close-up of the insect's legs tickling the air. In the bathroom, Eva searches the lino for moving things: silver fish or runaway beads. She picks up a dead shampoo bottle and holds it tight, tries to strangle it with one fist, but as yet she's incapable. Daily training is what's required. She can run and skip and squeeze her arms until they ache but she needs the help of something manly. Her father's bullworker lies across the towel rail. A grown-up slinky toy. She grabs the handles and eases out the coils. In front of the long mirror she sees a little girl with spaghetti legs and a thin-ribbed chest. This is the 'before shot'. She pulls until her arms start to judder. Then snap, she lets go before buckling into a heap.

'What's that noise?' Her mother is outside hovering like a hornet. The door hasn't a lock and there's nowhere private to develop her gangster accent and biceps.

'Nothing mum,' she says, putting the apparatus back where she found it.

She hears the sound of her mother breathing smokily through the key hole. Then the edge of her head appears round the door.

'Everything alright?' she says. She notices the bullworker and frowns. 'What's that doing here?'

'Must be Dad,' Eva says.

'You shouldn't be playing with that. It's your father's.'

'Look Mum,' said Eva, holding up her arms in a strong man pose. 'Aren't I strong?'

Alarm spreads across her mother's face. 'Don't do that Eva.'

'Why not?'

'Because it's not very nice.'

'I want to be a strong man in a circus.'

'Don't be ridiculous. Hurry up with that bath water. Your sister's waiting.'

She sits in a canopy of bubbles picking at her nipples, pushing them inwards and scaling her chest for hairs. At school in Miss Mason's class, they'd seen pictures of girls with rounded breasts and hips who ended up shaped like violins. Mrs Mason was a kind lady who talked about the future. When Eva threw Susan Penny's bag through the window because Susan Penny was calling her mother names, Mrs Mason listened to Eva's story and nodded like a vicar. Back in the classroom she said, 'In a few years time, all of you will begin to change.' Eva looks forward to it. She will become the 'Great Adolfo', dressed in a bearskin, scooting over a line of barebacked ponies. At the circus you could be a clown one minute and a strong man the next. Life lived in a caravan was life lived on your wits.

Standing on the cold lino, she drags a towel across her shoulders and smoothes down her curtain of hair. It was far too long for a strong man. She wipes the blade of the scissors free of the dots of bristle from her father's beard and starts to hack. In no time at all, her collywobble curls drift down to her feet. 'I'm gonna gecha Mrs,' she tells the mirror. Jimmy Cagney words leak out of the side of her mouth.

Her mother's make-up is scattered across the window sill, greasy with soap. She has a pencil somewhere, a brown to draw eyebrows. Eva darts the pencil across her chest, drawing dashes and squirls. Soon she has the most abundant chest hair she has ever seen. She slings the cotton bathmat diagonally over her shoulder and growls at the mirror. Outside, her mother is bashing the skirting boards with a hoover.

'Ready yet Eva?' she shouts.

The following day is Eva's eighth birthday. A fortnight ago, she made a list of what she wanted. Candles dripping on a rose pink cake, a pile of presents as tall as a door and gallons of fizzy pop that would explode down the back of the throat and stain her lips cherry red. But, so far, all that had materialised was a boiled egg, cooked just the way she liked it, and a trip to the beach with Patsy Lawrence, the next door neighbour, who wasn't a friend but needed to be looked after.

On the beach, Eva traces the path of the M4 motorway through the hillocks of sand as she sits crouched on the beach behind the windbreak. Meandering around the downy hills, she shunts a sandal carrying a bevvy of Barbies from pebble London to pebble Cardiff, where her Nanna (represented by a sandwich box) is waiting in her castle beset by dragons and rain. She squints her eyes against the light to see the outline of Patsy, throwing stones in the surf.

If only Mum would come back now, they could all have tea.

She said she was off for a walk but never came back. The girls dig holes in the sand and fill them in. Patsy slopes off to the icecream booth and returns with two cornets streaming down her hand. The girls lick the gloopy liquid from their arms to save it puddling into the sand.

'Don't worry,' Eva tells Patsy. 'She does this all the time. She'll be up with the tambourine-bashers, singing her heart out.'

'Why?' asks Patsy.

'It's her new hobby. She takes it up now and again, like knitting.'

'Church is for old fogies. You wouldn't catch me spending time there. Patsy wrinkles her nose in contempt. She is a slave to the Radio Times. Her ambition is to have a TV set in every room. 'She's funny your Mum, not giving you a present for

25

your birthday…' Patsy is a tall girl with a world-weary look, the first girl in her class to wear a bra. She wants to be a social worker when she leaves school. More than enough reasons for Eva to dislike her.

'Don't be so bloody horrible!' Eva shouts. 'She's giving you a good day out isn't she? You didn't have to come.'

Patsy is well aware of that. She could be at home watching an old black and white film. She says nothing. After all it is Eva's birthday and the poor little shrimp has a loony for a mother, who can't even buy her a present.

'C'mon I'll race you,' Patsy says.

'Where?' says Eva. Patsy scans the horizon.

'There,' she says and scrambles to her feet. She is pointing to the promenade where the dodgem stalls jostle with the hot dog stands and the mournful sound of a piano accordion lifts in the breeze.

They are off. Pounding the cooling sand, never even pausing on the rough patch where the pebbles pinch their feet and on to the stairs underneath the rusting ironwork of the sinking pier. Eva is sure her Mum will be here but there is no sign of her.

'I won,' trumpets Patsy. She is spinning on her bare feet, her skirt twirling round like a brolly.

They rove up and down the creaking boards for a while, whistling at the sea through the gaps, blinking at the flashing lights from the Spinning Wheel of Fortune, dreaming about hamburgers steeped in liquor. The crowd that gathers round the 'Jesus is King' posters wear dark ties and polished shoes; they look like a group of undertakers on holiday. The preacher is a big man with a rasping voice. He winks at the two girls and beckons them over .

'Friend of yours?' says Patsy.

'I don't know him,' says Eva scornfully. 'Mum probably

does. She knows all the evangelicals in this area.' They hum the tune of Rock of Ages, then drop down to their knees to search for lolly sticks,

'What's short and fat and can't sing?' whispers Eva, pretending to read from a lolly stick held out in front of her.

They look to the man with the hymnbook and snort like heifers.

When the sky darkens they know it is time to go home. 'We could take the bus,' suggests Eva.

'Aren't you worried about your Mum? She could be anywhere. Shouldn't we ring my house to tell them she's got lost?'

Eva's face closes like a clam. The last time her Mum had gone off, she rang the Police and Social Services poked their noses in; there was hell on for months. For two days her mother barricaded herself into the bathroom. The only glimpse she caught of her was of her feet dangling from the toilet.

'She can look after herself,' says Eva firmly. 'She'll be off buying my present.'

When the crowd starts to unravel, the suits drift away, clutching at their collars against the wind. Someone in the distance is waving. The figure is coming from the direction of the town and Eva knows it's her mother. Nobody else wears a coat that's such a striking shade of yellow. She's carrying something, a parcel or a present maybe, something shaped like a tube. Eva imagines herself scraping off the wrapping paper, delighting at the shiny something that lies underneath. But Eva and Patsy are rooted to the spot at the sight of Eva's mother. She has lost one of her shoes and her stockings are dirty. Her hair is trying to escape from her head.

'Hello there, girls. Had a nice time?' Mum's face is flushed. 'Haven't been too long have I?'

Eva and Patsy exchange looks in silence.

'Here we are love. The trouble I've had getting it.' Her mother wrings her hands in expectation. She is giggling to herself in a girly voice as she hands over a rolled up poster. Eva places it carefully on the ground and flattens her hand over the orange paper, smoothing out the torn edges. Her hand is trembling. It must either be very old or very special for her mother to be so excited. She's seen posters like this one before, outside the Methodist and Congregational on her way to school. The thick lip of paper is fluorescent orange and across it, written in letters as long as her arm, are the words:

What's missing from this ch__ __ch ?

U-R

Eva's mum throws back her head and roars, not like a lion or an ocean or a stream of traffic, but like a fire that cannot be extinguished.

Home to Roost
by Mary Lowe

It began with one small bag; an inconspicuous one, stuffed with a paint-stained jumper. Then a second one appeared. A pair of old trousers this time, dappled with plaster dust, and trainers, brittle and cracked. She watched over the weeks as the bags became bigger, their contents more elaborate. He stowed them in a gap behind the washing machine, but she couldn't fail to notice; she was training herself to be vigilant. She slipped her hand into the latest one and stroked the soft felt of a slipper. It was true then, her father was moving in.

The children were quiet at last, busy building a runway from playing cards. Outside in the garden, a trail of smoke wafted across from next door's bonfire. Through the haze Joni could make out the growing mound of rubble: salvaged bricks, smashed window frames, and the latest offering, slabs of formica, stacked like a deck of badly shuffled cards. He'd been salvaging rubbish from yards, meeting strange men on building sites who kept aside a bit of this, a bit of that, could let him have the lot when the gaffer wasn't looking. So the darkening hump grew taller. It was a mad structure, deranged. It creaked in the north-east wind, doubled up and festering like an old man, like everything he'd ever made. He'd shown her plans, spokes and wheel-rims sprouting from his sharp pencil. She'd stared out into the middle distance whenever he mentioned it.

'Up and on,' he said, flicking his eyes sideways at her for a hint of approval, but she refused to give him any.

The wooden hut could have been a den for the children; a shed for his tools even, but he was stuck on one idea: pigeons. The irony of the situation had not escaped her. Years ago she and her father waited for days at the pigeon loft for his best birds to appear in the sky and now they would look and listen together again, this time for the sound of a car, or the scraping of feet on gravel.

Joni pulled at her fringe and bit the skin from along her thumb. It was red sore. She needed ointment, but she didn't have time for that. If her father wasn't here to babysit soon, she would miss the bus and her wages would be docked. She twisted the wedding ring on her finger and prayed it would be a quiet night. Despite what her father said about Billy, she was still a married woman. And she took some comfort in that.

She checked her appearance in the tiny mirror propped against the window. Her cyclops eye, clouded with bronze, shone back at her. A disembodied ear appeared with its gilt earring catching the light, tawdry and bulbous; it was part of the uniform. Billy used to say she had lovely skin, told her not to wear make-up if she didn't want to be a tart, and now here she was, dusting her face with powder, clogging the crevices of her nose, plumping up her lips with magenta gloss. Magnet lips, Billy would have said, and told her to wash it off.

She shuddered the curtains across the window to block out her father's half-built monstrosity. The shed brought back memories of childhood: the sharp willow smell of the baskets where the pigeons were kept during transportation; the sharp stink of the nests as she felt amongst the feathers and twigs for eggs.

The room was like a furnace, with the gas fire raging. She walked out to the porch to cool down, craning her neck for signs of her father. The 'poor man's conservatory', according to Billy, it was full of plants, and the small patch of tiled floor was pocked with fallen leaves. Since Billy had gone, the porch had become a shrine. There were plants of all kinds with twisting stems, drooping flowers, sunlight-loving plants and hardy perennials. There were crocuses in flower, mini daffodils, jasmine trained around a hoop. It was a garden in a goldfish bowl for people outside to look into. Billy was proud of his plants. He liked to show off by using their Latin names. Acacia Armata, he'd say, Jasminum polyanthum, and he would talk to them as if addressing a legion of Roman soldiers. There was a pile of motorcycle magazines stacked on a shelf and a model of his Suzuki 250. The original was stored in the garage, muffled under a blanket like a sleeping canary.

She'd pinned photos along the wall: fluffier and rounder versions of Katy and Peter, holidays in Spain, a day at the zoo. The police had told her to make things visible. It's quite common for missing persons to observe the house for a few days before returning, they said. A man and a woman filled her front room, their uniforms stiff as cardboard, and told her that her husband was a missing person. Only days before, he'd eaten sausage and mash with the kids and shouted at the football on TV. She searched the faces of the WPC and her gruff male sidekick, but they spoke using textbook language and needed to be off to their next call. Time we must be going, they said in unison. We'll be in touch. That was six months ago.

She stared out into the breathing night where the telephone cable beat a rhythm on the gable-end. She tapped her fingers on the cold paintwork. There was only stillness. She laid a hand on his favourite jacket, hanging in the hall like a totem. Underneath it lay a pair of wellingtons, scrubbed clean and scoured for forensics. In the darkness, with her eyes squeezed half shut, she could imagine his outline; his nose, the square jutting chin, the blond hair falling forwards. She'd seen him many times over the past few months: a figure in a football crowd, a man with a brief-case driving at fifty through traffic lights, the top of a head in the bus queue. She felt in the pockets of the jacket for a clue - a bus ticket or a fragment of hair - anything which would hint at what happened, but the spaces had been turned out already; mined and catalogued. They were stored in a file held at the police station.

Today she couldn't bear the children to leave her sight, if she could have welded their hands together and roped them to her waist, she would have done. All three of them were rats caught in a trap, running across each other's hands and feet, trammelling the walls. They were waiting, always waiting, for news which never came. The room smelled of hot tarmac. The children's cries wafted down from the kitchen, cracking the stillness.

'What is it now?' She stood at the doorway to watch four-year-old Peter advance upon his older sister. There was a battle brewing. There had been a stream of tiny spats all day; the kids crying, teetering on a fault line, their cries pummelling the walls, the windows shaking.

'He's kicked me Mum, look.' And there was Katy with her self-righteous stare, showing off her skinny thigh with its tiny red mark. Joni felt her fingers flex, her guts turning liquid.

'But she's got my fireman,' shrieked Peter. 'She won't give it back.' And sure enough Katy's hand bulged.

'It's only a stupid plastic thing,' said Katy, her head jutting like a tortoise while she jabbed her tongue at her brother. Peter slid over to her, tried to wrench the plastic figure from her hand.

'Katy, I haven't got time for this.' Any minute now she would snap.

'Get off!' cried Katy, and slapped her brother across the legs

'That's it!' screeched Joni. 'Leave it, will you?' Her hand was ready. It might come down like a cudgel or a scythe or a sharp stab. She could never tell. She punched the arm of the chair and the pain in her hand ricocheted up to her shoulder. Katie glanced darkly at the floor, twisting her hair into corkscrews.

'How many more times?' Joni shouted. Her children smelled of bubble gum and static. They stood pale and unfurled, like plants without sunlight. Joni reached out to stroke Katie's hair, but her daughter flinched. 'It's alright,' she said softening. The shock of Katie's stare made her step back, lean a hand against the wall. She looked up at the ceiling, and breathed in, opening her chest until it felt as if she was sucking in a skyful of air. Her world was caving in.

At last, she heard the squeak of the gate, the key turning, the stiff hinges creaking in protest. A familiar voice shouted down the hall. Katie and Peter flew from the room like startled birds shouting, 'Granddad. Granddad.'

'Sorry I'm late pet. I got caught up,' said her father. He patted her shoulder and gave the children a hug. He'd brought chocolate, videos. The children clamoured round him like fleas dancing on a dog.

'You can say that again.' He'd come from the pub. She could smell it on him, the smell of danger; of slanty-eyed gossips who met over brandy and pep, and scraped at the air with their voices. She eased her jacket over her shoulders.

'Look, I've got to be off straight away. They've had their tea,' she said.

'Aye,' he was smiling. The lines across his face bunched together in folds. He was shrinking. Every time she saw him he looked thinner, more stooped. Sometimes he looked like all the other old men she saw on the High Street with rheumy eyes and toothpaste stains on their jumpers.

'I'll see you later,' she said softly.

She was back for midnight. It wasn't a good night at the pub. A new girl with brassy hair and hard eyes was asking questions. Are you married, then? How long for? What does he do, your husband? Her friend Martha had to step in and tell her to leave it. I was only being friendly, the new girl whined. Weeks ago, Joni had told Martha the truth about Billy, because Martha was involved with an alcoholic and had a face that pulled down at the corners. She listened in silence, shaking her head, her face grim. They spoke in low voices to make the words seem manageable. Disappeared. Vanished. Missing. The well-worn words twisted between them like a shroud.

Six months ago, Billy had left the house early saying he would be late home. They'd had a row, about Peter's shoes of all things, a pointless battle between laces and Velcro. Something complicated versus something easy. It's alright for you, you don't have to help him get dressed, she'd shouted, as he walked towards the car. He didn't come home that night, or the following night. Two hundred pounds was withdrawn from his bank account on the morning of his disappearance and by the end of the week the police had taken details of what he was last seen wearing.

She stood in front of the darkened house. She'd left it in a blaze of light - a beacon in an otherwise gloomy street. She always left the lights on, the windows sending pools of light onto the pavement. She pounded upstairs. Alive or dead? She played the game of Russian roulette as an endless tape loop inside her head. Sometimes she imagined a child snatch; a knock on the door, an engine running. Billy as a bogeyman, hidden behind trees, lurking in the shadows. But Katie and Peter were in their own rooms, two breathing mounds of blankets. The air heavy with the smell of cocoa.

Downstairs, her father was lying on the sofa, mouth open, drooling over his cardigan, wheezing. He'd always suffered with his chest, but as a younger man he worked in the foundry and lifted weights in his lunch break; built himself a body, strong as a horse. She was proud of him then and would wind herself around his strong legs; stand on his iron-tipped boots and be lifted around the house. Her father used to tell her stories about angels, flying creatures who had to pack their sandwiches in their feathers and didn't have to go to school. He told her, if she saw an angel, she was to make a wish. She used to wish things for her mother: a hat with a lolling daisy and a trip to Paris on a Bateau Rouge. Most of all, she wished that her mother could be like the other mothers and collect her from school, not lie around at home all day, gazing at the ceiling, snapping at barleysugar twists.

'Dad,' she whispered, her voice hoarse from the smoke from the pub. 'Wake up. It's late.' She touched him lightly on the shoulder of his waffle-knit cardigan, heavy as a coat. He'd had it for years. As a child, she'd thought it was woven from string. She remembered a time they'd gone walking along the river and it had started to snow. He wrapped her in his cardigan and carried her all the way home.

He opened his eyes, yellow-edged and clouded with sleep. 'I thought you were someone else,' he said. He pulled himself up and smiled at her. His face cracked into hollows, ' I must have been dreaming.'

'Anything nice?'

'No.' He rubbed the stubble on his face. 'I was dreaming about Billy. I heard a noise and, in my dream, it was Billy who'd come back to the house and he found me here, lying on his sofa. He was about to take a swing at me.'

'He wouldn't have done that, Dad.'

Her father heaved himself up by the elbow. 'Ah, but we don't know do we? There's a lot about Billy that we don't know.'

She bit her lip. They rarely talked about Billy these days. It was a hot coal between the two of them, anger seething just beneath the surface. Her father thought she was wasting her time. He's out there somewhere, he'd said, and he's not even phoned. What kind of a man would do that to his family? But she'd heard about people who just take off, who lose their memory, cannot cope with reality. She was prepared to forgive him anything. She just wanted him back.

'Joni love, there's something I wanted to talk to you about. It's my tenancy.' He waved his hand around the room. She'd wondered when he'd broach the subject. 'It's up for renewal,' he said. 'So I have to decide - no - we have to decide, within the next couple of weeks.'

She looked down at the floor and kicked the edge of the carpet with her foot.

'I can see pet, that you're not that keen on the idea, but you could do with the rent money, and of course I can help with the kids.'

This from the man who'd waited until Billy was gone before getting to know them. 'Not now Dad,' she said. 'What if Billy were to come back?'

Her father had never liked him. He'd warned her before they married. There's something not quite right there, he'd said, but each year that they stayed together, she regarded as a triumph.

She stiffened. 'Leave it, Dad. It's late. Some other time. I can't think straight.'

He shrugged and left her with the humming gas fire and half-drawn curtains, the street light shining an amber pool on the thin carpet.

By the time she came downstairs the following morning, the back door was open and the yard filled with tinny music from the radio. Her father was raking a saw across pieces of wood. Katie was outside crouched in her coat, practising with a hammer, driving small nails into a block.

'Look Mum, a hedgehog.' She held it up proudly.

Peter was sitting in the dirt playing with a piece of putty. He slammed it against the ground to make a better shape. He'd added beads for eyes, a twig for a beak.

'How's it going then?' She stuck her head round the door.

'Champion,' said her father, beaming. 'What a good set of workers I've got here.'

The pigeon loft was now three feet off the ground. It was an eyesore, a flatpack explosion, but the children had begged their grandfather to build it for them so how could she refuse?

She went to the front door to pick up the milk. There was something missing. Billy's jacket was gone. For a second, she had the ludicrous notion that maybe he'd come by to pick it up. She looked out on the quiet street half expecting to see him whistling cheerfully, his pockets bulging with presents for them.

'Kate, have you seen your father's jacket?' she shouted. But it was her father who sped round on his heels.

'Sorry, love, I just borrowed it earlier. Was a bit nippy when we first came out.' He reached out for the jacket that was lying in a pile amongst the wood dust. She snatched it from him. She hugged it to her. The cotton was cold and limp. In the daylight, she could see where the sun had faded it.

'Please, Dad, I don't want that jacket moved'.

'Sorry, love. I didn't mean any harm.' He hung his head. There was sawdust smeared across his face. He grinned at her and waved his hand over the pile of rubble.

'Granda's going to let me feed the pigeons when we get them,' said Kate. 'He's going to teach me how.'

'Is he indeed?'

'I'm going to become an expert and maybe breed a champion,' said Katie.

Joni glanced at her father, who innocently bent over a plank of wood, smoothing the end, sanding it down.

'We're getting them soon, Mum. Three pairs of birds.'

'You've never told me about this.' A line creased her forehead, folding it in two. 'You never mentioned birds. I thought you just wanted a hut. Like a monument, somewhere to store your trophies.'

He looked up, all innocence. 'No love. I thought I told you. You can't have a loft without birds. What's the point?' He chewed furtively on the end of his pencil.

'But three pairs? Why not one? You know the mess they make?'

'It's OK love. We used to have fifty pairs and we did alright, didn't we?'

She clung to the jacket. A hot stab of anger bubbled up inside her. 'Because you had me slaving for you.'

'You enjoyed it. You loved those birds.'

She looked into his sunken eyes, saw his scabby tat, the pitted nose. His lip stuck out like an emery board, his eyes were glassy. The older she became, the more her father looked like a rodent.

'You spun me stories. You said if I kept the pigeons clean, the Angels would give me the weight of muck in gold.'

Her father drew his eyebrows together and made his face into a puzzled mask.

'You didn't believe me, pet. It was just a harmless little joke, you knew it was.'

'Did I ? So why did I load that stinking, slimy stuff in carrier bags to take home to weigh it on the bathroom scales? I kept a tally: two pounds, three pounds; it mounted up. Not that you ever noticed.'

Her father extended his hand towards her. 'Look love, you're getting yourself all upset. It was just a harmless little story. It was years ago.'

'You don't know how much crap people will swallow Dad.'

She'd never asked him about the woman with golden hair and pearly face. It was years ago. She must have been about six or seven, but she'd never forgotten it. One evening, she was down at the lofts, watching the blue-grey sky for the homecoming birds, craning her neck to the clouds and sniffing for rain. She sat on an upturned crate, wondering why it was always her job to coax home the winners. Her father said she was the best; that they could picture her pretty face and it would guide them in. He'd gone to do an errand, he said, and would be back soon. She was combing the air for Bluey, the champ. A speck of movement up above only proved to be a starling. She might be waiting for hours.

Two figures arm in arm were coasting down the road towards her. She recognised the man as her father and, at first, she thought the woman must be her mother. But as they got nearer she saw it was a stranger, a tall blond with crepey hair and a mouth like a letterbox. As soon as they saw Joni, their arms dropped away from each other and the woman gave her father a kiss on the cheek and walked back up the hill.

Everything changed between them after that. Her father spent less and less time with his pigeons. In the end he sold the plot to a man who turned it into a scrap yard. Joni and her mother were left alone for most of the time, wondering when he'd be coming back from the pub or trips to see his friends. He never told them where he went. Joni spent long evenings sitting in front of the television, trying to block out the sight of her mother hacking at her own hair, and thrumming at the table top with discoloured nails.

Years ago.

At midday they ate waffles. It was a family tradition. She walloped the eggs and flour, beat out the lumps and stirred in milk to make a batter before pouring it into the mould. The smell of burning wafted through the house.

'C'mon you lot. They've been ready ages.'

They trooped in solemnly, panting, her father mumbling about a good morning's work, the kids with roses in their cheeks. They rubbed their hands together and held on to the radiator.

'We're going down to the animal auction next week, Mum. Going to choose our birds. Want to come?' Katie's eyes were sparkling. The outdoor air was doing her good.

'I don't know, love. It's a bit difficult. We'll have to see.' She glanced over at her father and Peter, who were wrapped in that helpless love-filled state she knew so well from her childhood. She felt a wave of anger kicking against her throat.

The waffles sat on the plate like pieces of scorched wood. They sat crunching in silence, their gums spiked with the sharpness.

When the front door bell sounded the children were finishing off their toast. They stiffened and were about to run for the door, but Joni told them to wait. Something about the cold air, the way the wind battered at the tarpaulin outside, told her that something was going to happen that day. She told them to wait, to finish their breakfast. She would deal with it.

Her father was half out of his seat. 'Are you sure?' he said.

'Trust me dad.'

She opened the door to the police. This time, not the young woman with the hairless arms, but an older woman, who was matronly almost, and a middle-aged man with a beard. They stood like cardboard cut-outs, their chalky faces framed by neat hair.

'Mrs Marchant.' It was bad news, she knew it.

The woman went on, 'I'm WPC Cole and this is my colleague, PC Daniels. We've got news of your husband. Could we come in?'

She was talking in a sympathetic voice that sounded incongruous coming from a uniform. Joni stood aside and they stepped into the hallway, blocking out the light with their navy blue bulk.

'I'll get you a cup of tea,' she said, and she showed them into the front room.

In the kitchen, her family were sat where she'd left them, like petrified mice.

'Well?' Said her father.

'Don't know yet,' she said. She went back in carrying a tray.

They were standing. All the available chairs were stacked with clothes or toys. She hadn't had the chance to tidy up. She moved a pile of ironing and made a space for them. She clutched at the soft clothes and the police officers sat down on the sofa in front of the streaming window.

'He's not dead,' said the male officer. 'Ehhh.' He drew his breath in sharply, exchanged glances with his colleague. 'There's no easy way to say this,' he said, looking at her intently. 'We've had a sighting in Bradford. Someone recognised him from a poster in the Big Issue.'

She gasped and sank back into the chair.

'Bradford.' She turned the word around in her mind. Why Bradford? She imagined Billy on the streets of Bradford, all those mosques, the Yorkshire accents. It was a long way from home.

'We've been to interview him to confirm the sighting,' continued the woman 'and I'm afraid...' she paused just long enough for Joni to realise that there was worse to come, '...he's cohabiting with another woman. They've been having an affair for a while.'

There was silence. She looked from the woman to the man, hoping they could offer her some kind of explanation.

'We're very sorry, love. We can't pass on his address to you at the moment, but the Child Support Agency will be getting in touch with you. We've notified them of the change in circumstances.'

'I don't know what to say.' She felt as if she'd been hit with a brick. So that's it? He's just shacked up with someone else?

The babble from the police radio poured a torrent of hiccups into the room. The next case had to be attended to. The police officers sipped their tea and left, handing her a leaflet explaining about victim support.

After the police had gone, she raged quietly on her own in

the front room; pulled at the raw skin at the side of her thumb. She tugged it with her teeth and tasted blood. There were eczema spots covering her hands. She had to get away from here. She'd been a sitting duck for too long. First her father, then Billy. They thought they could come and go as they pleased and she would always be here. A tap on the door made her look up to see her father standing, hands in his pockets, body bent like a bow. An old man now, needy.

'What did they say?'

She wiped her eyes. Prickles were burrowing under her eye-lids. He looked so expectant, eager almost.

'The usual. They just popped round to see how I was doing. There's no news.'

'I thought…' Her father ran a hand through his hair. 'Right. So that's that then. We keep hanging on.'

'Guess so, Dad.'

She went out to the porch, unhooked Billy's jacket, took one last look at the plants, the boots, the photographs, before taking them one by one and putting them in a box. The jacket was still damp from the morning. She'd leave it a while before adding it to the pile. The wind outside was bending the bushes into the shape of a cloud. It was time to make a bonfire.

A New Life
Janine Langley McCann

Grandma Thomas rented a tall narrow house on an old brick terrace that was long overdue for demolition. Two weeks after her mum's funeral Lesley Thomas got a phone call asking her to go over there, so she nicked a pound note from her dad's wallet, took another day off school and got a bus to the Leeds

City terminus. From the terminus, she cut up by the canal to the estate. She passed two blokes tipping in sack-loads of rubbish and a half-dead dog bound up by the legs.

'I'll report you for that,' she said.

'Aye, an' I'll chuck you in an'all if you don't shurrup,' one said, and he meant it.

For a minute, Lesley took a look at herself from their point of view, in the old rain Mac she wore to cover her shape, that practically fell off her bony shoulders. The thick black hair that cloaked them hung in greasy bootlace trails from the want of a good wash. A kind spring sunshine should have warmed her bloodless face, but only served to make her look more like a walking corpse. She stared the men out, but didn't push it.

Her grandma's house was at the bottom end of the old terrace. The little street was a cul-de-sac of sorts, in that a factory wall had been built along the end of it and the adjacent streets, linking all the bottom houses together. The few people left in the neighbourhood had complained that they'd never asked permission from the council to do that; they'd just put it up. The top of the wall was lined with broken glass and barbed wire, the face of it a host to every graffiti artist with a spare bit of paint. Gigs 4 Bev- Billy B 4 me- I heart John by K- West park secondary are slags etc. And the art: tits, cocks, fannies, couples fucking, and in such detail that live models must have contributed to a great deal of it. Lesley's mum had gone to her grave a good Catholic, her idea of sex education more or less amounting to, 'Always sit with your legs crossed, and never put anything strange in your mouth.' Much of what Lesley had learned in life was down to that wall.

When she arrived at her grandma's, the door was locked. Her bladder was heavy. She rapped on the door a while then went around the terrace to the back gate. That was also locked. So she put the dustbin up to it and climbed over into the yard. Her gran's house still had an outside toilet. This was one time Lesley didn't curse the fact. When she got back round the front, the neighbour, Mrs Greenall's door stood open, so she gave it a knock and stepped inside. She could hear her grandma and Mrs Greenall nattering through the back, but she didn't dare go through. The Greenalls had a huge black mongrel that went for your legs and she couldn't place where it was.

'Hiya Gran,' Lesley called through.

The dog started then, 'Oof! Oof! Oof!' from the kitchen.

Lesley froze by the front door.

'Shurrup ye daft bugger!' Mrs Greenall yelled at it. There were several brisk wallops to the barrel of the animal's carcass, then just muffled growling from it.

'I'll be with you in a minute,' Grandma Thomas shouted, then on she went, nattering. Her voice was spiked with irritation.

Lesley waited by the door, wishing she'd not bothered coming and feeling queasier by the minute. Mrs Greenall's Dad, unrattled by the dog, was kipping in an old armchair by the window, his chin resting easy in the remains of breakfast on his threadbare jumper. Spring sunshine filtered through mustardy stained nets onto the old man's head; a seeding spud, baking in its thick yellow light.

'Sit yourself down, Lesley,' Mrs. Greenall shouted through.

The dog barked.

'Thanks,' Lesley called back, but stayed put.

Apart from the chair the old man was in, the only furniture in the room was a fake leather sofa. Two holes, gouged roughly out of the arms of it, served as ashtrays. Scorched treacly foam welded each mass of tabs into one lump. Lesley looked away from that, only to focus on a sticky fly trap, hanging from one naked bulb, centre ceiling, where, amid the mass of corpses, the latest catch wriggled out its protest at a slow death.

Lesley felt herself swaying. Her shoulder jarred hard against the edge of the open front door. Pain rampaged through her back like an angry mob. With cold sweat on her brow she staggered outside for air, missing the step and stumbling into the street. She was on her back, staring up at the sky, when her grandma came out, looking angry and anxious at the same time. Mrs. Greenall followed her, then the dog, sniffing at Lesley's out-turned baseball boots.

Mrs. Greenall took charge, kneeling over Lesley, who looked blankly back up at her. She slapped the girl's face to one side, then the other. She said, 'I think she's alright Ivy. You have a go.'

Lesley strained away from the woman's breath, stale and sweet like the waft from an old cake tin, but it was in the back of her throat by then. With some effort, she shifted onto her side and wretched. Barely anything came away, just a thread of thick spit that clung to her face like the fly on the trap.

The two women got Lesley into her grandma's house, then Mrs. Greenall left. Grandma Thomas made tea in frosty silence, but when she came back to the front room, her manner had thawed a little.

'Here you are. Get that down you.'

Lesley sat with her legs up on the couch, beneath a huge framed print of two lion cubs locked in play. She took the tea, not really wanting it, to keep her gran happy, so she wouldn't start. But then she tasted it, and her tongue loved the sugar so much that she all but scalded her throat gulping it down.

The old woman sat herself in the big armchair with the

crocheted valance over the back and wiped a creeping tear from her eye. Some of the baggy skin there stayed dragged to the side. She sniffed, looking straight ahead, out through the nets, to the red brick wall opposite. Lesley didn't know what to do. She'd never seen her grandma cry. She thought she should go over, maybe put an arm around the old woman. But the body in the big chair, under the shiny cardigan, looked alien to her, like stone in a silk sack. Grandma Thomas wasn't the kind of grandma you cuddled. After a silence the old woman blew her nose into a man-sized chequered hanky and then sat back, sipping her own tea from a china cup.

'You want to get yer sen sorted out lass. You look like a right state. Like a bloody gypsy, dressed like that. Get yer sen some bloody meat on your bones an' all. You look like a skeleton.' When she lifted the cup to her lips again, her hand shook. 'What've you been doing any road? Sittin' round all day long. You want to get yer sen out and get a job lass.'

Lesley's cheeks blazed. 'Me Mother's just died, in case you hadn't noticed.'

'Aye well, it's not gunner do you any good sittin' round mopin' all t'time, day in, day out. Not gunner bring her back, is it? Sittin' round mopin' all day long. Liggin' in bloody bed 'til all hours.'

'You couldn't even be bothered coming to her funeral, you.' Before she'd finished saying it, Lesley was crying. She put her hands up to her face, as if she was holding it together.

The old woman didn't flinch. 'No good payin' respect in death to them you had none for in life, I say.' She sipped her tea. 'All them times, she were happy enough to palm you off on me. Never forked out a penny mind, but could I ever ask her for owt? Could I 'ell-as-like. Not once. Look at when I did me hip and needed a bit of shoppin' and stuff. Yer dad came. Oh he did alright. He's a good lad, our Brian. Do owt for ye.

46

Ask her for owt and she'd look down her bleedin' nose at ye.' She stuck her nose up, to demonstrate.

Lesley turned cold. She didn't want to talk about her mother any more. Not to Grandma Thomas. Grandma Thomas had never wanted her dad to get married in the first place. Not to anyone, her auntie Pat had said. Lesley wiped her face on her sleeve. She said, 'Anyway, I can't get a job yet. I'm still at school.'

Her grandma's cup came down heavy into the saucer, rattling it. 'You never bloody go! When's last time you went?'

'I go all t'time. Anyway, me Mum's just died', Lesley repeated, but louder, ' in case you hadn't noticed.'

The old woman talked over that. 'About twice in t'last year that's how many times. You might as well get yer sen out lass, get a bloody job. There's plenty of jobs. There's that new supermarket just down from you. Cryin' out for staff down there they are.'

'I thought you hated bloody supermarkets…'

Her grandma turned to glare at her, face on. 'Don't you go swearin' at me lass.'

'…said they're putting all t'little shops out of business. That's what you're always going on about.' She did her gran's voice, but whinier, 'Want shootin' them bleedin' supermarkets do, nya, nya, nya.' She turned her face up to the lion cubs, but even from the corner of her eye she could see the old woman bearing up to crack her one. So she thought she might as well earn it. 'Anyway, they've banned me. For nickin'. Two jumpers and an Arctic roll, this last time. Said I'm not to step foot in there again as long as I live.'

The old woman drew back a long breath that Lesley never heard come out. Clutching the arms of her chair she pushed herself to her feet, then walked stiffly across the room, past Lesley, into the kitchen and through the door to the foot of the stairs. Her footfall was slow as she mounted them. And then nothing. Lesley sat, waiting, listening, but there was no sound at all from upstairs. So she stayed sitting for just long enough to let the tea settle in her belly, then got herself up to go, making one last trip out to the toilet before the long walk back to the bus terminus.

It was May, and still the toilet was cold as a crypt. Lesley shivered, but stayed sitting there, long after she'd squeezed out the last drop, just thinking. It was as she passed back through the kitchen that she heard banging, from upstairs at first, then closer, heading downward, gradually, towards her. She could hear her grandma coming down with the noise, struggling, breathing hard, clattering something against the narrow walls of the stairwell. There was a 'ching'; shrill and metallic. Finally, the door at the bottom of the stairs gave under the onslaught of a small slippered foot, and there she stood, cradling it in her arms like a long lost child.

'Give us hand here,' she panted.

Lesley helped her to the kitchen table with it. It was old, black-enamelled, with raised-up keys on stems like spider legs. They dropped it onto the plastic table cloth, 'ching', then both stood back, just taking it in.

'I didn't get you over here for this,' Grandma Thomas said, 'But you might as well have it. It's a damned good piece of machinery that.' Her voice was thick from crying, but the tone was calmer, like all the fight had gone out of it.

'I can't type,' Lesley said.

'Well you can bloody-well learn, can't ye.' The old woman was walking away, toward the tall cabinet in the corner. 'That was my mother's. She worked, durin' t'first world war, when you'd no choice. It's a solid piece of machinery, that. Worth a lot of money. You make sure you look after it, d'you hear?'

Lesley said, 'Yeah, 'course I will,' but she was more

interested in the brown paper parcel that her gran was taking from the top shelf of the cabinet. It was criss-crossed with string, which meant it was important. There was also writing on it in thick biro. As the old woman came closer, she could see it said LESLEY in big capital letters.

Grandma Thomas lifted her hand, slapped the parcel lovelessly into it, then launched headlong into what she had to say. 'This is it. You understand? That's all there is. There'll be no more. You understand me? I'm not gunner be around much longer now. They expected me gone months ago, long afore yer mother went. T'others 'ave had theirs, so don't go givin' any away to them. You understand? Give nothin' away to no one, right? Especially to that bloody numb-skull ye've been swannin' about wi'. He'll have every bloody penny you've got if you show him a farthin'. You put it somewhere safe, alright?'

Lesley didn't look up from the parcel in her hands. 'He's buggered off,' she said.

The old woman breathed a sigh that sounded overly satisfied. 'Aye well, it's not like nobody warned you about him, is it. Eh? I told you he were no good, didn't I? How many times? Got sick of hearin' me own bloody voice, I did. Anyway, it's a blessin', mark my words. Now you go take that and get yer sen some decent clothes, lass, then put rest away safe, d'you hear? Ye get yer sen tidied up an' go get a good job. And learn thi-sen to type. You can't go wrong with a trade. D'you hear me? I'll not be around long now, I tell yer. Few weeks at most.' She grabbed Lesley's arm, making her wince. With each word she shook it. 'So you take care, and take care of that money, 'cause there'll be no more. D'you hear?'

Lesley nodded. 'Alright... Thanks.'

The old woman let go of her and breathed a final long

sigh. She'd finished. At last. 'Now,' she said. 'Your dad says you've summat to tell me.'

Lesley put the parcel deep into her coat pocket and picked up the old typewriter. 'It doesn't matter,' she said. 'I'll get off. Go look for a job an' that. You take care, Gran.'

By the time she reached the front door, the old woman was back in the big old arm-chair, with the crocheted valance over the back, staring silently ahead. Neither said goodbye.

Lesley hauled the typewriter as far as the spot where the two men had been tipping into the canal. The bound-up dog was floating in scum on the surface, close to the edge. It's head hung so low in the water that on first glance it appeared decapitated. Grunting, Lesley lifted the typewriter away from where it had been resting, on the tiny bump under her over-sized Mac. The baby kicked furiously, as if in protest at the removal of the vast weight from it. Leaning out over the water, Lesley took aim and dropped the typewriter onto the floating dog; a bull's-eye shot, sending it down with a thick 'glump'. It was out of its misery. No doubt now. Then she knelt, spellbound, as a thousand tiny bubbles rose and popped on the surface in an endless stream: dog words, dog dreams, last wishes. Until through them came the dog itself, urgent, cold-eyed, like a man at war, sending her scrambling back to her feet.

Her Favourite
by Janine Langley McCann

Tom Farrow stayed at his dad's house the night before they did what needed doing. It gutted Tom to realise that that's how he thought of the place now- as his dad's house, a place where even the soap needed a good wash.

They didn't take the walk over in the morning, as planned. It was drizzling and that seemed like reason enough. Tom sat channel-surfing in his dressing-gown until his dad, busying himself within eyeshot, said, 'What about two-ish, eh? Lunches are over by two-ish. Before probably. We could maybe set off about half one-ish - quart to two?'

'Two's fine,' Tom said, craning his neck to see past the old man to an ancient episode of Batman and Robin. Tara, their old Collie, took the movement her way as a gesture of goodwill and sidled up closer to Tom, who felt burdened by mixed emotions about her. He'd grown up with the dog and loved it still, but couldn't bear the smell that came with age and neglect. He ruffled the hair on the back of her neck, saw something move at the roots and pushed her to the floor.

Bill Farrow pretended not to see that. He said, 'Have you had any breakfast yet? There's cereal.'

'I can't be bothered Dad, y'know. I'm not a breakfast kind of a guy.'

'What about lunch. Have you thought about what we'll have? I've got ham in.' Bill reached across his son to prise a day old coffee mug out of its stain on the window sill.

Tom was aware of his dressing-gown falling open around him as he shifted his weight. He pulled it close to his legs self-consciously.

Bill swung forth his watch arm, spelling out the time. 'Ten fifty-two just gone. It'll be lunchtime soon anyway, so we'd better decide.'

'I'll get fish and chips, if you want,' Tom said. 'Save you cooking owt.'

'Aaahh, it's no trouble, no trouble. I've loads in.'

'Yeah, but I miss fish and chips Dad - proper ones like you get up here. If there's one thing you can't get down London for love nor money, it's a decent plate of fish and chips.'

'Not the only thing an'all, I'll bet.' Bill laughed a while to himself about that. Tom took himself off to get dressed while his dad was still chuckling away to himself, shaking his head. It was getting on for half past eleven when Tom, dressed, showered and shaved, unbolted the back door.

'I'll warm some plates,' Bill said.

Tom was shaking his head, pulling on his boots. 'Don't bother Dad. I like them out of the paper.'

'It's no bother lad. It'll take me two minutes.'

Tom looked away from him, through the frosted glass of the back door to the straggle of overgrown rose bushes that shadowed the small back garden.

'No, I really like it, y'know, the taste of fish and chips fresh from the paper. You don't get them in paper down London. It's all, like, polystyrene boxes and that. They don't taste the same. You can warm a plate for yourself, if you like, but I'll just eat mine out of the paper. Honestly.'

The walk took ten minutes and in heavy rain, but Tom felt glad to be out. He'd been gone from home just over a day and he was missing Deb. She was much like his mum had been: petite, pretty smile, always clean, always cleaning. When Tom had begun to realise he'd married a woman so much like his mum, he found he had to ask himself just how much like his dad he was. Still he didn't want to think about that, not now. He stepped up his pace, pulling the mobile from his pocket. There was another text message from America, from Peter, his older brother. He was sorry he couldn't get over. He sent his best. Tom needed to ring Deb. No signal, again - fucking hills, factories. Factories nobody used. Hardly anybody worked around here any more. They might as well tear the whole lot down. He'd find a phone box in the village. He took out his wallet. For some reason he had a powerful urge to look at his children. He opened his wallet, not knowing he'd stopped walking, and looked at his children. They were much older now than in the photo. It wouldn't be long before they had kids of their own. In the photo they both sat on Deb's knee; two boys, two years apart. Fair, blue-eyed boys. He wondered what kind of people they would turn out to be, in what kind of a world. Rain began to drip from the fringe of Tom's bowed head, drowning his family.

The queue at the chippy was out of the door. Waiting customers huddled under umbrellas. Tom didn't have one, but thought by then he couldn't get any wetter. There was a phone box on the corner, but he would lose his place in the queue, and by then the urge was thinning out. Tonight would be better. He'd have a clearer head, he hoped. On the way out of the chippy, Tom realised he'd forgotten the scraps. His dad had asked for scraps. Tom decided not to go back. His dad'd kill himself one of these days. A body doesn't need all that fat.

'You haven't got me scraps.' Bill was scanning the contents of the opened paper on his lap.

'Aw, I forgot. Sorry.'

Bill put half a fish between two slices of buttered bread and bit in. 'Best scraps you'll ever taste, them. Lovely in a sandwich. Get some bread.' Morsels of food passed from his open mouth to the pile of bread on the coffee table before him. Tara followed their trail, sniffing the stacked bread. 'Gerro-o-off.' Bill waved his sandwich at the dog.

Tom kept his eyes on the TV. 'I like these teacakes from t'fish shop. It's ages since I've had fish in a teacake.'

'Well there's plenty of bread if you want it.'

Tom wolfed down his sandwich, not realising how hungry he'd been, then felt sick. He sat back, bloated. Tara jumped on to the couch, finishing what was left in his paper.

'I was wondering,' Bill said, 'If it might be better to get doctor down. I mean, she more or less suggested it in t'first place. It were her that started ball rolling.'

Tom pushed back his hair, then looked at his hand, then smelled it. He was covered in grease. 'Look…' he lost his thread for a moment. 'Can we just… can we just stick to what we said? Look, I'm off to wash my hands, then we'll get off eh?'

'Aye. Whenever.'

Tom soaked the soap in hot water, then let the water out before he washed his hands. He picked up the flannel to wipe the sink round, then sniffed it and threw it in the bath, then he washed his hands again.

They stepped out into the rain, which had steadied off to a drizzle again. Bill shut the front door behind them. He swung out his watch arm as they set off walking. 'Thirteen forty-two. Loads of time.'

'Are you really taking the dog, Dad? Couldn't we just leave her here? She'll be alright on her own for a bit.'

'No, no, no.' Bill patted Tara. 'They love dogs over there. Any animals like. They do. They've a budgie, y'know.'

'Well have you got a bag?'

'What for?'

'Y'know. In case of emergencies. There's signs all over, Dad. You can get fined now. Fifty quid.'

'That'd have to be some pile that.'

Bill went back in the house to get a bag. Tom walked slowly on ahead with Tara, who promptly squatted on the path to relieve herself of the weight of left over fish, chips and mounds of bread and butter. Tom at first tried to drag her by the lead to the gutter, but that just seemed to spread her mess across the pavement. Over the road an elderly lady frowned through her window at Tom, who smiled in a helpless sort of a way, blushing and shrugging his shoulders.

Bill told Tara she was a good girl while he scooped her waste up into the bag. Tom wondered if germs could get through plastic. He walked on ahead again. When they reached the main road at the end of the lane, Bill took the bag of dog dirt out of his coat pocket. Tom saw the top of the pill bottle, in the same pocket, and felt his face redden. The lump that had been building in his throat all day threatened to swell up and choke him.

Bill said, 'There's a bin over there. I'll just get rid of this.' The top of the bag was open. As they crossed the road Bill swung the bag, increasing his swing as they approached the bin, letting it sail from a few feet away. 'Bullseye!'

The bin was mounted on a lamp post. The bag went bottom in but not all the way, the open top sagging down the side. Part of the contents slid out and dropped on the pavement.

Bill ran toward it.

'Don't!,' Tom shouted. 'Don't get it on your bloody hands. Just leave it for God's sake.'

Bill stared at his son. 'What's up wi' you?'

Tom felt his eyes filling up. He turned away from his dad. 'You won't wash them,' he said. 'I know you.'

Tom was still holding Tara's lead. In true Lassie fashion she looked up at him, whining, wagging her tail, like there was something wrong that maybe she could fix. Tom wanted desperately to stroke her, but couldn't. He needed to keep his hands clean, for Mum. When he was small and he'd been to the toilet, she'd hold his hands in hers, first smelling the palms, then over, inspecting his nails, and she'd smile, always. Tom was a good boy.

Tom felt his dad's hand on his back. He stiffened.

'It doesn't matter,' Bill said.

'It matters to me,' Tom said, and walked on.

They stopped at the corner shop by the church. Tom bought her dandelion and burdock, her favourite.

When they reached the nursing home, Bill swung out his watch arm. 'Fourteen-twelve just about. A bit longer than we said, but never mind, eh.'

The atmosphere inside felt to Tom like a huge tropical toilet. The smell was heavier than a rain-sodden dog. He'd forgotten. It'd been just weeks, and he'd forgotten, or put it from his mind.

They could hear her screaming from the ground floor. You recognised your own. When they got this bad they didn't bring them down to the communal areas of the ground floor. Up in her room a male orderly was holding her tiny body while the nurse straightened out clean sheets on her bed. The nurse looked at Tom and smiled.

'She's not really in that much pain,' she said. 'She only thinks she is.'

Tom, his head full of his mother's screams, wondered what the difference was.

When they put her back in the bed, she calmed down. She saw the two men in coats by the door and held out her hands, moaning, confused, but showing signs of recognition.

'We've given her a bit of a clean up,' the nurse told them. 'We'll give her a good bath later, after you've gone.' She left them alone.

Tom rushed to take his mum's hands. He didn't know what to say. He told her he was Tom and she nodded. Bill sat by him on the bed.

'She's still got stuff all over her from dinner,' Tom said. 'Don't they clean her properly?'

Tara strained to get up on the bed, but Tom stopped her. She kept her front legs up, reaching to lick the old woman's hands, resting in Tom's.

'They will later,' Bill said. 'I mean, they do.' He stroked wisps of his wife's hair. Her hair had nearly all gone with the last dose of drugs. 'They don't know what they're sitting in,' Bill went on. 'It's the dementia. They just feel summat, so they have a feel around y'know. She doesn't know what she's doing.'

Tom looked again at the stuff under her nails - brown, thick, like chocolate, and in her teeth as she smiled at him. 'Oh God,' he said.

Bill picked up the hands his son had dropped. He squeezed them tight and his wife lay back against a stack of fluffed pillows, drifting back into her own thoughts. She looked perfectly relaxed, except for her eyes. Her eyes stayed full of anxiety, as if she could see a train coming, and coming, right at her, but never quite getting there. Tom turned away.

'Let's clean her up, eh?' Bill said. 'Get her looking something like.'

He went into her bathroom and began to fill the sink with hot water, squirting in some body wash that Tom had sent her for a present. He soaked and wrung out a flannel which he brought to the bed. He gave it to Tom who was sitting, head in hands, staring at the door. Tom took the wet flannel and studied it. He smelled it. It smelled of roses. That seemed to kick him into action. He got up, turned and smiled at his mum. She spotted him and smiled back. The two men took off their coats. They did an hour's shift on the cleaning, in and out of her tiny bathroom. They brushed her hair. Tom took a bottle of her favourite perfume from his rucksack and dabbed it under her jaw line and on her wrists where she liked it. Bill had bought her favourite magazine at the corner shop and the two took turns to read the fiction pieces out loud to her. Tara snuck clumsily onto the foot of the old woman's bed and fell asleep. At sixteen twenty-two, Bill Farrow swung out his watch arm and said it was about time to go. Tom emptied a tumbler of pink stuff down the sink and used the cup for the dandelion and burdock, and the pills, which had to be popped open one by one. When the drink was ready, Bill lifted his wife's head. Tom kissed her on the mouth and told her, 'It's your favourite, Mum. It's Tom. I've brought you your favourite.'

Beau de L'air
by Susannah Rickards

One morning, among his dad's bills and his mam's prize draw notifications, there was a letter for Euan. He stood in the sunny hallway, in his school shirt and underpants, and opened it. A black-edged card inside announced the funeral of a Tracey Marie Alleyn, next day at 3.00 pm, with refreshments afterwards at 27 Crewdson Drive, Collingwood Park. Underneath a message had been added by hand: *it would mean the world to us all if you could come.* He examined the writing to see if he recognised it but he didn't. Boxy letters in blue biro, a style he associated with his nan, with elderly women who never venture opinions. Nice touch. He was pretty certain there was no such person as Tracey Marie Alleyn. He'd never heard of her. This was some scam set up by Ritchie and Jason to trash his first date with Helen. Euphoria had made him stupid; he should never've told them she'd finally agreed to go out with him.

"Les Enfants du Paradis. It's, like, a special screening," he told her, "somewhere called the Literary and Philosophical Society." He hoped the name of the venue would impress her. It impressed him. But she said, "Yeah, I know the Lit and Phil. My dad lectures there sometimes."

"It's got subtitles."

"Mmm, that'll be fun." She always sounded like she'd just swallowed ice cream. He never knew if she was taking the piss. She had this way of looking at him the same way she looked at puppies wriggling on their backs in the park, like he was endearing and beneath her.

"OK," she said. Then, as if it was a line in a teen movie: "Pick me up Tuesday, school gates at four."

In the kitchen his dad was up to his usual: cutting all references to the Royals out of the morning paper so their smug-arse faces wouldn't spoil his breakfast read. His mam was buttering herself some toast, but as soon as Euan walked in she offered it to him instead. She was too subservient. Euan'd tried to tell her.

He still had the post in his hand. On the off-chance he asked, "You know the Alleyns, Collingwood Park Estate?" His dad worked at the Leams Cigarette factory, just past Collingwood Park. Maybe it was possible someone'd got the name wrong and it was meant for him. Three of his dad's mates at Leams had died of emphysema only last year, but his dad shook his head, saying, "Yer gin soaked old sow," as he shredded the Queen Mum's gummy grin onto his growing pile of offcuts.

"You coming to this goth gig at the crem the morrow?" Euan asked Jason as they hiked the steep shortcut up the bluebell bank on the school side of the dene.

"What?" said Jason.

"Tracey Marie?" Euan waved the invitation at Jason, who took it and stared, shaking his head.

"Divvent kna. Never heard of her."

Euan glanced at him. He could just picture J and Ritchie ambushing him from behind a gravestone with a water-pistol jet of Thunderbird wine, suckering him for standing Helen up over their phoney invite, but it didn't look like Jason was bluffing. Master of the deadpan voice he might be, but when J tried to lie his eyes always squinted. They were dead straight right now, concentrating on keeping his balance. The climb was making Jason puff asthmatically. He preferred the bus but Euan enjoyed forcing him to walk occasionally - Jason needed trimming.

Not J and Ritchie then, but something was up. As he was walking through the lower school, this gaggle of girls jostled past him and he heard them whispering, "Euan" and, "Tracey Marie." They kept turning back to stare at him, giggling nervously, but when he called out, "Oi, yous, come here. What you saying?" they scarpered. Then Don Bird, Head of Studies, had caught Euan as he came out of assembly and whispered, "A word in my office at twelve, Neilson. Good lad." Bird was always a tad theatrical, but he'd looked at Euan with such concern, dipped his voice so gently and gravely that a lump had formed in Euan's gut. What had he done? What was wrong?

It was a pisser. He'd planned to meet Helen at lunchtime, so he could intervene if she tried to change her mind about their date tomorrow, but she'd be in orchestra practice by the time he got clear of Bird. He'd told her he wanted her to look over his essay on L'Etranger. God, he loved watching her read his stuff. Loved how she sprawled on her stomach on the school field, her chest almost touching his sheets of scrawled A4, kicking her legs up in irritation when she disagreed with what he'd put, so her skirt worked its way above her knees; how her hair fell over her face, glittering dark and giving off the smell of almonds, and how, when he tried to nuzzle her, pretending he was just reading over her shoulder, she swatted him away like a fly. Like his ideas were too important, too absorbing to be distracted from. And then she'd attack those ideas one by one with her slow, assured voice. She liked a good intellectual slanging match. There weren't enough lasses with brains, but he'd found her. Helen pulling books off the shelves in her parents' cavernous house, in vigorous pursuit of some John Donne quote, was the image he sent himself to sleep with every night, and he'd decided months ago he was going to glue himself to her till she got bored of fending him off and said yes. He even sort of loved that she made him wait, though he'd had to keep convincing himself she was keen underneath, that she'd give in soon. And now she had. But he'd not get to Helen this lunchtime. Don Bird's summons sat like a cold pebble in his stomach all morning, making him wonder.

Another weird thing: at break he'd been on prefect duty by the first form bogs, shooing out the smokers, confiscating their tabs, lamenting that the little tossers smoked Regal cos they were cheap, not decently filchable tabs like Silk Cut or B&H, when he'd noticed this dwarfy kid lounging against the radiator at the far end of the corridor, staring and staring at him.

"Oi, outside, you," Euan had said, which the kid ignored. Instead he approached Euan furtively, and when the kid was no more than a foot away he blurted like an accusation - "You're Euan Neilson. Fuckin be there, all right!" - his face filling up with colour at his own audacity - then fled.

Euan'd never set eyes on the kid before, but he noticed the home-made black arm band tacked to the sleeve of his blazer.

Don Bird kept him waiting twenty minutes. The bell for second sitting at lunch was just sounding as Bird appeared in his doorway with the school secretary and two sulking history teachers. "Nightmare curriculum," Bird was placating them. "If I could choose between being dragged over broken glass by a galloping donkey or timetabling European Studies, I'd favour the donkey every time. Ah yes." He focused suddenly on Euan as the teachers mooched off. "Patricia Alleyn rang and asked permission for you to be excused lessons tomorrow. Of course, of course, under the circumstances, you must go, and er, Helen no doubt will take impeccable notes in your absence. So sorry to hear about Tammy Marie."

"Tracey Marie."

"Yes of course."

But who is she? Euan was about to ask when Bird's phone rang.

"Bugger, bugger, excuse me," said Bird, loping over to it, hand over the mouthpiece as he picked it up, to add for Euan's benefit, "Actual derivation: Bulgarian heretic, so not half as satisfying an expletive as one might wish. Who the bugger am I talking to? Oh, Headmaster, hello." With a wink, Euan was dismissed.

So next afternoon at three, he was not an hour away from an evening alone in Helen's company, but on his way to the crematorium, with his hair gelled back, and his school uniform on because his mam had said just cos it was technically all black didn't mean he could consider for one minute wearing what he'd come downstairs wearing. She'd made him an arm band, and he'd borrowed the black tie his dad had got for the emphysema spate last year. For some reason he couldn't tell his parents he didn't know the girl. He lied and said he'd been asked to represent the school, and they'd looked proud.

He'd never been to a funeral before. No one he'd ever known had died. This was still true. His dad had looked up where the crematorium was on the map, and Euan took the bus up the coast road, which skirted Collingwood Park. He knew the estate a bit. A couple of years ago he'd gone back there late at night quite often, to the houses of friends of friends after Leams Factory Under 16s discos, before Iggy Pop and The Clash, before Helen, when he was still into Northern Soul. The houses were tiny and posh, oppressively clean and full of rules - shoes off in the storm porch, no smoking, coasters under your coffee cups - but there was always a Jack Russell who clamped your leg and pumped himself against it, as if the dark desires these houses suppressed could be ejected through small pets. Had Tracey Marie figured on one of those evenings? Was she the sister of one of those lads? Had he snogged her once at Leams and forgotten?

The bus dropped him right outside the gates, but the cemetery driveway went on forever. Ahead in the distance the crowds were already thinning under the concrete colonnade of the crematorium entrance, heading inside. He was late. He broke into a jog. The sun was strong - his black shoes soaked it up, making his feet feel tight inside, and the heat itched his skin under his blazer, but he reckoned he'd best not take it off. A couple of lads his age were planting up flowerbeds, barebacked, so that just for a moment he wished he was them.

The chapel was packed. In a tiny ante room off to the left, a coffin stood on a blue velvet plinth. In front of it four girls in his school's uniform, but much younger - second, third years, maybe - were sliding nasally through an acappella version of a chart song:

"Come show me your kindness
In your arms I know I'll find it
Oh Lord don't you know with you
I'm born again."

He slipped in the back, shirt wet to his skin under his blazer, trying to take silent, shallow breaths, but his chest was tight from running and he couldn't stop himself gasping. A couple of heads turned, nodded sympathetically, a tissue was passed down the row to him.

"It is always difficult to accept the Lord's claim on our loved ones, never more so than when they are taken from us so very young," the vicar began, as the four girls pleated themselves together and keeled back up the aisle to their row, their cheeks striped blue with mascara.

"We want to shake our fists at him up there and shout: 'Why?' But it is not for us to dwell on why the Lord has needed to recall Tracey Marie so tightly to his bosom, but rather let us celebrate the life she had here on earth. And what a full one it was. I don't believe I've ever seen this chapel so packed. To each of us here, Tracey Marie was special, remarkable. She has left an indelible, joyous impression upon each and every one here." Rows of heads in front of Euan nodded vigorously, sniffed, let out choked chuckles of agreement.

He learned a couple of things from the vicar's eulogy. Tracey Marie had been a pupil at his school; she'd died of leukaemia last week at the age of 13, after a long brave battle. He tried to conjure a picture of her in his head, some thin pale girl with purpled eye sockets; thought perhaps he'd seen someone around like that. Then the curtain was closing in front of the coffin and the chapel's PA system was whacking up Elton John's "Song for Guy." It was 3.30. He should be in double French Lit now, with a direct view onto the netball courts where Helen had been playing centre forward for the past half hour. Perhaps if he slipped out now, was lucky with buses, he could get to the school gates in time and surprise her. He'd not even spoken to her to cancel - had to leave a message on her parents' answermachine.

He half stood to go, but saw that the family had begun a formal exit from the front pews. Barrel-shaped women, crippled at the waist, sober-suited men, their hands comforting and steering the shoulders of their wives. Behind them, head so bowed his neck looked stretched for execution, was the minute kid who'd confronted him in the corridor the day before. The brother, then. His eyes flicked from side to side as he walked. They landed on Euan, and his brows raised slightly, as if to say, "You're here. Good on you." As the family drew level with Euan, Tracey Marie's brother tapped the woman in front of him and said, "Mam," pointing him out to her.

"Euan, pet?" Grief had pouched her cheeks, made her eyes round and red. She looked like a guinea pig. "You'll come back to the house?"

Back at the house, everyone knew who he was. "Euan, lad. You can handle a beer?" Too composed to be her father, must be an uncle. The man handed Euan a can of Tennants. Another man with the same gently sagging jowls, his skin grey, stood stiff-backed at Tracey Marie's mam's side: that'd be the dad. The air was high with furniture polish, and the gassy smells of snacks being heated in the kitchen. Euan moved to the closed window. On the sill were formal portraits and enlarged snapshots. Tracey Marie. He was right. He'd definitely never seen her before. She was white as meringue, moon-faced. A fat kid. In the earlier pictures her thin blonde hair was combed excruciatingly tightly into bobbled bunches that jutted above her ears, drawing attention to the width of her features. In more recent ones her head was covered - gypsy scarves that made her middle-aged, a floppy velvet hat with a drooping purple rose. If he ever had a kid this happened to, he'd get her to show her baldness, not coddle the world from it with these desperate disguises. But in every photograph she was grinning. Real grins, not put on for camera. He noticed the spots of light bang centre in her pupils. And in these later pictures her skin, though bloated with chemo, had a sheen to it.

Some relative bustled up to him bearing a tray. The hot

eggy and pork pie smell was too much. He bolted away from
her into the hall. The four girls who'd sung were sitting on the
stairs, arms wreathed round each other, sniffling, sucking
cans of Panda Cola through straws. They gawped as he came
through. "Eeh, God, looka, it's him," one of them whispered.
He had to climb past them, he wanted the bog. Four pairs of
eyes swivelled to his progress. Like a hydra. One teen beast of
mourning. "Can yous shift?" He sounded gruffer than he
meant to. His calves brushed their narrow shoulders as he
passed.

What must have been the bathroom door was locked. The
door adjacent had two white tiles glued to it, the ones you get
in Whitley Bay gift shops, printed with flowers and names,
first Tracey, and underneath, Marie. He pushed it open. The
room inside rushed at him. The rosy flush of the wallpaper,
the duvet cover, the curtains, seemed to tint the air pink. A
gang of pastel fur toys picketed the bed. A vanity table was
crammed with lace mats, perfume bottles, red and mauve
plastic love-heart photoframes. He'd never seen anything so
asphyxiatingly feminine. Girlie bedrooms. God, he was
seventeen and he'd never been in a real one like this. He'd sat
around in Helen's room sometimes, along with Jason and
Helen's mates, but hers was crammed with books and sheet
music, wooden masks on the walls, more studenty than
girlish. And he'd never courted any other lass long enough to
get invited back, just snogs on the Leams dancefloor, on
doorsteps, at bus stops.

A familiar, incongruous object caught his eye. On a
painted school desk under the window, on top of a stack of
Jackie magazines was a Bantam dual-language Baudelaire.
Unlike his own copy, this was immaculate, the spine still
shiny. It had barely been opened. Beside it was a stack of the
dead girl's school exercise books. Looked like she decorated

them. The top one was coloured in felt pen. Over and over, in deft bubble lettering, she had graffittied every inch of the cover with his name.

Right down his body, his skin turned cold then hot. He pushed the top book so it overhung the pile. The one beneath was emblazoned with him too, this time in lightning zigzags. And the one below that with tiny lettering that spiralled out in a continuous flow: EuanEuan'meEuanNeilsonTraceyMarie NeilsonTraceyMarieNeilsonEuan'n'TraceyMarieNeilson 4evaneva. And on.

He went to the vanity table. About half the framed photos were of him. Out of focus, long distance shots of him on the school playing field; him, J and Ritchie on their way to school, heads down, tabs to their mouths so they looked like a cover shot for some band; his head, the size of a pea, cut in a neat disc from what had to have been the expensive school group portrait of the lower sixth. Under the protective glass table top, between two doilies, was a pristine copy of the page from the local paper that featured him when he won the junior division of Durham University's French translation prize. It stared up at him. He remembered at the time a self-consciousness creeping in under his happiness at getting the prize, because the photographer fussed on so long. When the item had come out, he'd examined the shot briefly, critically, and then forgotten it. But in this bedroom it looked cocky, capable of more than Euan really was. What had she seen in him? How could she covet that lank hair, that beaky nose? Why, as he now saw she had, had she traced the photo onto fine paper, and blocked in the panels of light and shade, making a Warhol icon of his face? There were several attempts, in different colour ways, tucked neatly against the mirror. She'd labelled each one: Euan in green and gold; Euan, reds; Euan, homework: a study in monochrome. The one she must've thought best, she'd framed. Euan in purples and blue. It endowed him with a louche, Jim Morrison edginess.

Who did she think of when she thought she thought of him? He needed to know. He searched the room now, swiftly, methodically, his heart quicker but his head insistent. He uncovered a padded diary with a flimsy sweetheart lock, easily snapped, and a scrapbook. He took them to her bed, with the few photos of herself she'd bothered framing. He shoved the cuddly toys onto the floor, took off his shoes, his blazer, loosened his dad's tie. He skimmed the pages of the diary first, searching only for his own name.

"Today I told Miss Darrick I've changed me mind. I want to do French not Spanish. Euan does French A level. Je t'aime means I love him."

... "Gold star day!!! Saw Euan. On a Saturday! Lord Jesus I thank you. You shine on me. I was in Jean Genie's on Percy Street and he went into Thorne's bookshop right opposite! I made Lisette follow me, left Donna lying on the floor screaming we'd promised to help yank up the zip on her jeans. I stood Right Behind Him, honest to God. He wanted this book called Bo de Lair. It's French. They didn't have it. Lisette said after it means something like *Lover in the Sky*. (That is so dead beautiful.) She does french already The Lucky Bitch. But back to Euan in Thornes. He was wearing his denim jacket and his dead faded Wranglers. I nearly died. And then Omigod! When he turned round He Saw Me. He Looked Right at Me and He Smiled."

He read right through, every mention. One entry cross-referred him to the scrapbook. She'd been hanging round his house when he was out. "It's georgous," she wrote. "It's all covered in tiny stones. I picked some off the walls, so now I have a Bit of Castle Euan in My Room!" She'd actually sellotaped tiny bits of pebbledashing from his house into the book. A couple of the stones were still there. "Had a row with dad," she put. "He won't have the house done with pebbles. He says we're not a seaside B&B. I called him a cheeky pig. I heard him telling me mam the new drugs were making me nowty."

He felt gorged when he was done. He went back again, and slowed down, reading some of the bits between. Hospital visits were perfunctory entries. There was scarcely any self pity. The most he got was when her mother had bought her a teddy bear, to cheer her up because she'd cried at the pain after the bone marrow transplant. She seemed uninterested in her sickness, unthreatened by her brief future. She wanted a life like Euan's, with Euan. She wanted to run her hands through his long tangled hair, she said. She'd even learned a couple of lines of Baudelaire to quote for him - none of the caustic sombre stuff he favoured, he noticed. She'd homed in on Elevation. Love, happiness, making your body take off, like flying.

Gutsy girl, he found himself thinking, searching for some of her racier bits to re-read. She wasn't ashamed of anything she wanted. Thirteen, but she'd put: "I'd do anything with that Euan. And I mean Anything. Honest to God. My top would come right off!" And there was another long section devoted to the top button on his skin tight cords, and what might be underneath. This little lass, writing like that because of him; thinking, well, as lads do. He never knew girls could think that way. He looked at her photos again, at her plump white child's flesh, her benign, bald head. Tried to imagine it, taking the blouse off her. How willing she said she'd be. How it might be nice after all, to have all that marshmallowy flesh, those doughy half-grown breasts wanting him, joining in, instead of Helen's lean, restless, rejecting body. His stomach flickered. He rolled onto his front on her bed, breathed in. It had that hairspray and sweat smell of the cheap perfumes the girls from Leams wore. What a wonderful smell. He was lying there, holding the best photo of her, the one which showed her as far down as the waist, when her dad walked in.

"Son?"

Euan looked up. His face was burning so hard he felt feverish, headachy.

Mr Alleyn came and sat on the bed at his side, bringing into her room the stale car smell middle-aged men emit. Euan's own dad had it.

"You divvent need to get up," he said. "It's all right son. I understand."

But Euan sat up a bit, cupping his hand over the broken clasp of her diary. He'd been lying there, talking away at Tracey Marie in his head, he realised. Mr Alleyn had interrupted them. The things he needed to tell her were so crowding his mind that they blurted themselves out to Mr Alleyn instead.

"She's good at art. It's a bit tidy, but it's gutsy, y'kna?"

Mr Alleyn nodded.

"Her writing's too neat though." God, that came out shite. He glanced at Mr Alleyn, but he was faced away from Euan, staring out into her pink room.

"What I mean, like: some people are so stupid they reckon if you write that neat you haven't got a brain. Tracey had a brain."

Mr Alleyn didn't reply. He suddenly buckled where he sat, and expired noisily. Shit, what've I said? I've upset him, Euan thought, but then Mr Alleyn righted himself, with a blue rabbit in his hand from the heap Euan had ousted. He put it on the bed. Stooping and straightening, sighing with each exertion, Mr Alleyne reinstated her toys one by one. Euan

70

shifted off the bed to give them room. He came and knelt at Mr Alleyn's feet to help, passing the animals to him. When they were done he straightened up and hovered in front of Mr Alleyn. It was impossible to leave the room. He swallowed.

"Em, actually sir, I didn't know her at all."

Mr Alleyn looked up at him. There were flecks of white skin in the bags under his eyes.

"Aye, son. I kna." He reached for Euan's hand and held it, squeezing intermittently, stroking Euan's palm with his thumb. "I kna that feeling very well."

The Paperback Macbeth
by Susannah Rickards

Recall a room. This is what Joseph instructs himself to do each time he wakes. Not just the anchors of furniture but the very dust and clutter of a given day. It's a trick he heard of years back, in conversation or in a magazine, on how to keep your mind. How not to rock yourself and sing your way to endless blankness.

He's already rediscovered each room of his grandmother's house where he grew up; her chicken coop where he collected eggs; has passed hours rediscovering the details of classrooms and lecture halls around the campus where he obtained his teaching certificate, and has returned to his schoolroom, his beloved, tranquil place of work. Each day so far he's been able to suppress the urge to cheat his self-imposed rules and recall the outdoor ceremony of flowers and fires, of drums and fried chicken that announced his marriage to Njeli. But he may allow himself to recant because of last night. He was woken again by the banging of metal doors, the dragging sound and stifled cries. They are working their way down the line of cells each night, getting closer. Last night the sound was too near, next door perhaps. Next door but one, no further. His neck is rigid now, its muscles are like lines of fire flaring up into his skull. Today he will treat himself and use his mind to go home.

A door opens in from the yard. To his left is a pale, paint-flaked wall. A portrait of Our Lord, blue, pink and gold, in a narrow frame, hangs centrally, fixed by a nail. Definitely a nail not a hook - he banged it in himself. Njeli was outside at the time, pounding maize, her hoarse, low voice repeating the alto part to a local hymn: nasadiki, nasadiki, ninasadiki. Don't go to her, he wills himself. Stay in the room. Below the portrait stands a cupboard, grey-painted and spindly-legged. Its door sticks. Njeli swears as she yanks at it, and he scolds her. Inside: two tumblers and a serving bowl. The top of the cupboard is where he sets his briefcase each day on his return from school. He puts it down, opens it and removes the sheaf of essays, stacks them as a reproach to himself should he later think of sloping off for a beer before he's marked them. Ah yes. Also inside the cupboard, at the back and wrapped in old newspaper, is a small bottle of grain liquor. His throat scalds at the memory when he finds it. He closes his briefcase and puts his paired shoes close to the open door out of kindness to Njeli.

The cupboard has a drawer. It holds a paperback copy of Shakespeare's Macbeth given to him by a British actress from the troupe that visited their village and performed in his own school hall. He was given it when he went backstage after the show to apologise for his fellow villagers. They'd catcalled Macduff in the final battle and pelted him with mealy-meal, refusing to leave the hall with Macbeth slain. He was supposed to be the hero - what sort of play was this that

72

leaves its finest warrior dead? When the actor playing Macbeth stood up shakily for the curtain call, they leapt like a football crowd and whistled and cheered.

"Macbeth is the name on the poster," he apologised backstage, "so he has to win."

The actress who played Lady Macduff - so sweetly - turned from unwinding her blue head-dress and laughed.

"I am Joseph Mutabe, Teacher," he told her. "It was a very fine performance. Very fine."

She held out her hand to him. "Thank you. Perhaps you should offer them all a class on the text."

He bared his palms. "I am the teacher, and even I have no text."

"Oh!" Her tiny inbreath. That was a detail he'd not forgotten. She'd turned from him and when she turned back, the book was in her hand. "You must have this."

Her own copy, with the lines for Third Witch and Lady Macduff underscored faintly in pencil. "Please," she said. "I'd throw it out anyway. There's only four more shows. We're flying back next week."

"I'm obliged."

And then she shook free her long red hair, and combed it with her fingers, saying: "Macbeth has the finest poetry ever written, don't you think? She should have died hereafter...so beautiful. Not even Lear touches it."

He wanted to pull up a chair right then and talk more, their thighs not quite touching, but she was called away by the Stage Manager in his British army shorts, keen to get the set dismantled. From the doorway Joseph watched her, high astride the scaffold battlements, unscrewing pipes and handing them down to King Duncan and Donalbain, and then, when the castle was down, wrapping swords in velvet cloaks, stowing them in a trunk now bound for England. Take me with you!

How quickly his mind has veered off-course. It's not so easy to concentrate today. Last night's noise has furred him, like a hangover. He returns to the room. The corner beside the cupboard is bare. He runs his eyes over it, finds it dusty, but this is wrong. Njeli is a meticulous housewife. He wipes it clean, begins again at the corner: a stretch of plain wall and dirt floor brightened by the plastic weave mat. Against the wall a little further on is their bed that doubles as a settee by day, spread with a knitted blanket and folded kikoi cloths.

Njeli is sitting on it, hands on her knees, her marvellous knees as broad and firm as melons. She clicks her tongue when she sees him, about to begin that conversation again: She didn't marry a man of education to live in a shack. Where is their television? Where is their good settee? Why does she still cook over a fire on open ground like her mother and grandmother? Joseph has tried telling her that any spare money from what he earns should go towards little Joseph's education and although he's no more than a melon pip yet inside Njeli, she says, "What? So he too can fool some poor girl with pretty words and tie her to life in a shack?"

"Njeli," he says, "The wealth of life is in here. I insist you listen." He has the copy of Macbeth in his hand and opens it at an earmarked page. "Art thou afeard/ To be the same in thine own act and valour/ As thou art in desire?"

She interrupts: "Oh, Mister Shakespeare, you are so good for my beauty sleep. Nothing make my eye close faster." She leans forward to reach under the bed for something, so close to him now, he can smell the oil in her hair. It's a magazine - no, a catalogue for one of the big stores where the misungu buy stuff. She opens it and smoothes the page.

"Mmm hmm," she says melodiously like she does when they're dancing. "This is so nice." She has her hand on a picture of a sofa. She isn't looking at him. "This looks so very comfortable for relaxing."

Outside his cell there is a clink of metal, the sweat spreads cold across his back and Njeli is gone. The hatch at the base of his door springs open and a tin food tray is shoved inside. He tries to stay where he is but the fatty bones from the guards' meal last night are already in his hands and his house has gone now too.

Another room comes to him. General Fulam's library. High ceiling set with two wooden fans, a walnut table which gleams so immaculately that the school exercise books spread open on it look improper. The walls of books made Joseph clammy with envy when he was interviewed here, but he knows now that if you try to pull Paradise Lost from the bookcase, ten inter-linked trompe l'oeil book spines, hollow inside, will accompany it. Joseph sits on the plumpest sofa. General Fulam's children stand on the carpet before him.

"Let me hear it again," Joseph says and they respond in soft singsong, "Tomorrow and tomorrow and tomorrow/Creeps in this petty pace from day to day..."

To his brief shame Joseph has timed this recital with the return home of the General whose boots are clipping down the hall as they begin. Joseph hears them pause at the open doorway. He doesn't turn round but concentrates on nodding and mouthing encouragement at his charges.

"Can you tell me the metre of this verse?" Joseph asks when they reach a breathless, "sound and fury/Signifying nothing."

"Iambic pentameter, and, um, feminine endings," Khosi, the daughter, parrots. He knows she has no real idea what this means although he has tried to explain: how the five iambs echo the natural rhythm of thought in the English language, how the extra syllable fractures it in moments of intense distress.

"Correct," he smiles at her, satisfied these alien literary terms will impress their father, who doesn't pay good money each week to have his children privately educated in things he himself already knows. Today Joseph is going to suggest, when he sips a mean dose of Scotch malt with the General, that the children enter for the School Certificate in Advanced English. It is a most prestigious examination but it would require extra tutorial hours. He is still three hundred and eighty shillingi short of Njeli's sofa. To soften the General, he has planned a surprise. The boy, Bosi, has learned by heart Macbeth's final valiant speech and Joseph has added some warrior moves to accompany it.

The General enters the room, pinching his nostrils. "Are they progressing well, Teacher Mutabe?" he asks. Joseph leaps to his feet. "Ah, General Fulam, you are home." The General grunts assent. He stands more than a head taller than Joseph so that Joseph's eyes are always level with the red and gold decorations of office across his chest. His pale green uniform is never darkened with sweat. Joseph feels crumpled in his presence.

"Bosi has a new piece," he offers.

"We'll hear it then."

The boy takes his position on the carpet and Khosi retreats to her father's side. He puts his arm around her.

"I will not yield/To kiss the ground before young Malcolm's feet," Bosi begins. His legs are too splayed, his gestures stiff and wide. Joseph winces. The General's face is set. He listens to the end. There is a pause. He steps forward, his hand raised to the boy, and Joseph feels himself lift onto the balls of his feet, ready to shoot forward and interrupt the strike, but the hand lands on the boy's head and roughs his hair. "Excellent, excellent," the General is saying.

It is gone seven by the time Joseph leaves. He has missed the bus that stops at the foot of Daniel Bundu Avenue, where the General lives, and it will be quicker to walk into town and catch a bus to the village from there than to wait for the next. Perhaps he will go via the market and pick up a chicken for Njeli. The General has agreed the extra lessons. The sofa is a few weeks nearer.

Joseph cuts down the broad grass bank that raises Bundu Avenue from Central Boulevard below. At his back are the fat white houses of the Embassies, the homes of government and military officials with their sprinklered lawns and street lamps. Below him, the scuffed pavements of the city, the dull glass roof of the market and beyond it, the square. He half notices the yellow and red banners hanging there, the mill of people, the bulk of grey army lorries in among the traffic, but his mind is still on the General. It is a baffling thing. When he enters a room Joseph panics, and yet the man is always civil to Joseph, more civil than he would expect. Today they took their whiskies into the garden and sat a while. "To learn by rote in this way has many benefits," Joseph tried telling him. He is anxious to stress the wider application of studying English Literature. "It improves the mental faculties, increases the powers of concentration, can even - " he sipped, decided to chance it - "prevent the deterioration of the brain in later life."

The General stared at him. "Teacher Mutabe," he said. "Poetry is a pleasure, no more, no less."

"Yes sir."

"It is a pleasure no life should be without."

"Of course. Indeed."

He has the chicken now, ready plucked, dearer than the feathered birds, but it's a convenience Njeli will appreciate. It is wrapped in paper and warm under his arm. The sun is still hot on his face and his mouth thirsts for a beer. The reds and yellows of the protest banners flash in his peripheral vision but he is keeping his eyes on the bus stand ahead, not turning towards the square. Then his name is called, clearly, three times. He picks up his pace, feigns concentration.

"Joseph!" Suleiman is in front of him, grinning, a bulging laundry bag strapped across his chest. He holds a placard of Daniel Bundu's head. A black X has been painted through it, obliterating the President's eyes, nose and jowls. The word FREEDOM is printed beneath, each letter tall as a hand. "Brother!" Suleiman embraces him. The corner of his placard nests lightly on Joseph's shoulder. "I knew I would see you here."

"Brother," Joseph replies.

"Will you take a petition round?" Suleiman asks. "We're missing people coming out of the shoe factory. Here - " He delves in his laundry bag among the bundles of pamphlets.

"I'm late already. Njeli worries."

Suleiman stands back from him. "I haven't seen you at meetings for a while."

Joseph shrugs.

"But you are here now." Suleiman presses his hand. His palm is warm and dry, but behind the smeared lenses of his glasses his eyes are unblinking.

"Suli - I teach long hours."

Suleiman looks past him, at the crest of Bundu Avenue's hill, where General Fulam's house stands.

"So I've heard."

"I have obligations."

"Yes, Brother, you do. Take the petition." He fishes in the bag and pulls from it a clipboard of curling papers, holds it out.

Joseph stands there.

"Sign it, at least, Brother Speaker."

This is a savage reference. From a long time ago. The silly passions of college boys. Life is not so cut and dried as Suleiman would have it. But Joseph takes the clipboard, signs, returns it, faces his friend. Suli looks at the signature.

"Your name is not as clear as it once was."

And before Joseph has time to reply, his head is bagged, the chicken knocked from under his arm, his feet are off the ground. He hears Suli's muffled cry: "My name is Suleiman Saeed. I live at twenty-two Park Buildings. My name is Suleiman Saeed. I live -"

You call out your name. They used to practise it in meetings. Your name and where you live, so passers by will remember. So some good stranger will go to your home and tell your family why you haven't come home. Joseph opens his mouth and it fills with the dry dust of the hessian over his face. His body is hurtling through the air. When it lands one twisted foot hits the metal floor of what must be an army van, but the rest of him is cushioned by bodies.

Njeli is smiling. She stands in a circle of purple flowers, ground-nuts and eucalyptus leaves. Torch flames flicker around her. Suleiman and Njeli's brothers lead the dancing. Smells of spiced chicken and grilled maize are in the air, and Njeli's uncle Adi with the gold teeth, who no-one had seen for six years, has come from the coast with an enormous fish that spits on the grill. Njeli's dress is a miracle, a white satin robe with a turban that appeases her desire for a Christian wedding and Joseph's own bid for tradition. It is late in the evening and her skin is pearly with heat. Now it's time for him to kick aside the eucalyptus leaves and crush the nut shells under foot. To break the circle and free her into his arms. He is prolonging this moment. He is no longer Joseph Mutabe, primly westernised teacher of English language, he is a bridegroom. And the wall of noise, of hooting and chanting that wraps him, comes from the throats of people who love and know him. Her eyes are on him, her mouth is split into the broadest smile he'll ever see. He steps forward.

The door clangs. This time the dragging sound is made by his own tied feet pulled across the earth corridor outside his cell. The mutant squeaks are from his own lips. Where the blindfold gapes across the bridge of his nose he makes out faint green light from an army lamp. Bolts are drawn and his toes now clog with gravel from the yard. The air on his face is so sweet and fresh he is glad of it. Even in this moment. His heart and lungs push at the cage of his chest and his blood is swifter in his veins. This is the final sensation of being alive. They tie him to a post. The meaty sweat of the soldiers who bore him retreats. The air is still. He feels the heat of urine down his thighs. He waits.

The quiet is broken by the measured click of boots across the courtyard. Then a voice: "Name?" and a soldier's reply: "Joseph Mutabe."

"Teacher Mutabe, heh?"

"Sir."

"Hm." The speaker pauses. There is the sound of a metal catch opening, a rustle, then a clipping noise. A flare. Joseph flinches. What are they planning? The rich scent of cigar smoke fills the air. His body loosens. A hand brushes Joseph's lips: the cigar is being put to his mouth. His throat is so dry, but he sucks in, obedient. The smoke is delicious, fragrant and savoury. His mouth had forgotten such possibilities. Then the smoker leans in, so close Joseph can smell his cologne. Quietly he says, "They gained distinctions in the Advanced Certificate of English. Both of them. I thought perhaps you would wish to know."

General Fulam.

Suleiman would spit now, or curse or burst into

revolutionary song. But Joseph's last words are, "That is gratifying. Thank you."

The boots retreat and the thud of soldiers' feet follows. A conversation is taking place on the far side of the courtyard. Here he is, tied to a post, the last waters of his body ejecting from every pore, and the gunfire doesn't come. The sad, hot stench of his own fear rises to his nostrils, jolting him.

"Please?" This is his own voice, foreign to him now. His tongue is thick, unused to speech, but what has he to lose?

"Please? General Fulam, sir?" He pitches the words across the courtyard. "What is happening?"

The soldiers thud towards him. He's being untied.

"Kiss God's arse," one of the soldiers says. "It's not your time. You're being moved on tonight."

He's crouching on a cold hillside. Soldiers threw him in the back of a van and drove for hours. He was turfed out here, his hands untied and a water bottle placed in them. A rifle was pressed into his spine as a soldier said, "Don't move till you can't hear the van anymore. Then you can uncover your eyes. After that, it's up to you." The rifle jabbed him. He heard them climbing back in, the van doors slam, the engine start. One of them leaned out and called to him over the revving: "If you get to the sea - village called Kawesi, someone there knows you. So I'm told." Dust spurted over him as the vehicle pulled away.

The sun is coming up and turning the greys to gold and green. The tiny spiders crawling over his feet, biting his flesh, have scarlet bodies and orange legs. In the distance light prickles over a wide stripe of water. Such colours. He sees now that the rooms he'd recalled in his unlit cell were muted in his memory. Colour is astounding.

Someone knows him. Someone knows him. He stumbles

downhill. His body is weightless. It's as if the mountain shunts him downwards; his legs play no part. As the sun grows, small blue and yellow lamps of flowers shine up at him and he follows their lead until the mountain hits a track and a row of shacks comes into view at the edge of that band of light, painful to the eye, that must be the sea.

An old man squatting by the side of the track at the edge of the village stands with agility as Joseph approaches. He stares calmly at Joseph, then turns his neck and calls: "Adi! Adi!" He continues, but his dialect is so strong, and Joseph so unused to words, he cannot decipher them. A figure appears at a doorway and comes forward to greet him.

Njeli's uncle. Adi. The one who brought the fish to Joseph's wedding - the only time Joseph met him. And yet this is the man who knows him, tipped off by Lord knows who - Adi won't say, just lifts his head in a tired grin, displaying the gold of his mouth - and leads Joseph down to the sand to rest. Adi sets a bowl of tomatoes before him, so ripe they burst out of their skins and fall apart in Joseph's hands. He is grilling a side of tuna over a fire on the beach. The light is too enormous now. Joseph sits with his back to the sea, head down and feeds the tomatoes into his mouth.

"No," Adi insists, "you mustn't go back. You must now take a boat."

He prods at his catch with a stick, poking away at the fish, the fire. And he explains. There is no village to go back to. There is no Njeli. No little Joseph. It happened months ago. Adi's voice has tired of emotion. His story comes out flat, like something that happened to strangers. Soldiers came, they destroyed the crops, slaughtered the livestock - didn't even take it for food - and torched the houses.

The schoolroom too. He wraps some fish in a leaf and puts it on Joseph's lap. The charred flesh stings Joseph's thigh. His mind will not grasp the news, it flows through him like water. "This is not possible," he tells the uncle, but his body flushes hot and cold and he can't move his hand to the fish. Njeli. His schoolroom too.

"Eat," Adi says. "Still, we must eat, where there is food."

Joseph sits.

Uncle Adi turns back to his fire and spears a piece for himself. Unless Joseph plans to give himself up again to Bundu's army to starve and rot in a pit, he is saying, then he must listen. He must leave the country tonight. Adi has found him a place on a boat. It is a well-run route. And costs twelve thousand shillingi. Adi will pay for now - in honour of his niece - to ensure Joseph's safe crossing and good quality identity papers. Joseph can send the money when he gets to Europe. It would be better, of course, if Joseph had a friend he was visiting in Europe, someone who would stand for him as guarantor because he will be arriving without funds. They may send him straight back. Does he know anyone?

"Of course not."

"No-one from your teaching days? No penpals? An educated man, and you never bothered to make contacts in Europe?" Adi clicks his tongue.

The actress who played Lady Macduff appears to Joseph, turning to face him, one hand untangling her blue turban from her long red hair, the other outstretched, holding the book. On the flyleaf is an address in England, but the lettering is faint and hieroglyphic. It slides out of focus. Now she sits on her stool on the makeshift stage in the village hall, leaning forward to stroke her children's hair, teasing them that their father's a traitor, as the Murderers appear in the doorway behind her. The over-ripe tomatoes he has eaten shoot from his gut onto the sand. He crouches, spitting, coughing. Uncle Adi puts his hand on Joseph's shoulder. It seems the gentlest gesture Joseph has ever known.

"Joseph? No-one?" Uncle Adi says.

Joseph lies down on the sand, his arm over his face to protect his eyes. Njeli is sitting on the bed-settee, smiling up at him, she carries little Joseph high in her belly - a sign of good health and vigour. The money for her real sofa is in the drawer of the grey cupboard, tucked inside the paperback Macbeth.

Occasional Large Print
Betty Weiner

After pleasuring herself she slept again, hands relaxed across her ribs; a dreamless sleep this time, without any pain; a weightless blanket with no end or edge.

A knocking and a voice at her door intruded, woke her. Slowly, she turned her head, began to clear her throat.

'Sofie? Are you alright there?'

She pushed the duvet from her face and tried her voice, 'I'm alright.'

But a moment later, urgently - 'Mrs. Stone?'

She called, louder this time, 'I'm alright, thank you.'

'Righty-o then.'

It was the new Assistant Warden. Clearly, no-one had told her about knocking later on Sundays. The Warden never knocked before eleven. Probably everyone in Golda Meir House knew that Mrs Stone slept in on Sundays. Thinking about this made her smile. She opened her eyes, blinked at the flame.

'It's just a night-light,' she would say when the Warden remonstrated about the risk of fire. After all, people here lit candles for the dead all the time.

'It's too near the bed,' Mrs Barnett would pronounce.

Mrs Stone didn't explain that she lit it only on Sunday mornings and when she dropped off again it was into a sleep so still that not a thread, not a mote of dust stirred in her room for another hour.

The night-light was in a little cut-glass bowl Sam had given her for a wedding anniversary, their second or third. Fourth, perhaps. She couldn't remember. At the time she had been engrossed in a story about Mandarin China and was developing a yearning for jade. The bowl Sam found was a clear, pale green and underneath there was a silver label: Made in Bohemia.

The light from the small flame caught all the chiselled surfaces and provided an exotic aura for their love-making. And references to the flame or the bowl, to jade or to Bohemia became signals of desire, a private language in public, an invitation at bedtime.

When she reached for the matches, Sam was with her again, his fingers finely-tuned, his phrases seductive, unchanged. His eyes saying yes, yes. She stroked her own breasts and talked in Sam's voice, let him make love to her and finally, staring through him, called his name into the stillness of her small - but - big-enough apartment.

It suited her well. She could dry her washing in the bathroom and eat in the tiny kitchen. But the bed-sitting-room was spacious and this was why she had chosen Golda Meir House above the others. She had a small settee and an easy chair in one window, and a round table with three dining chairs in the other. She kept her old radio on the dining table. When she wasn't reading, she listened to Radio 4. Near her bed there was a door into a dressing-room, six foot by four and a half, with a wardrobe and chest of drawers, and a long mirror. She'd never had a designated dressing-room before.

There was space by her bed for a small round table which she'd covered to the floor with a linen cloth and a shorter, folk-weave one on top of it, as she'd seen in Housekeeping magazines. This was where the glass bowl sat, alongside tissues and Co-Codamol and water and a clock with a large, illuminated dial.

Her library books sat in heaps on the floor by her armchair, mostly biography and travel. Occasionally she accepted a volume in Large Print, but she didn't like doing this, not yet. Her stick, 'Handmade in Helmsley', a birthday present from her grand-daughter, hung at a slant on the back of a dining chair.

In Golda Meir House all the flats were the same design. Like houses that are identical on the outside, she would say, you knew whose home it was by the style within.

Thursday evenings, Sofie Stone played Scrabble with Edith and Freddy Hill in the flat next door. She'd push a week's worth of newspapers to one side of the settee and make space for her sherry glass on a table covered with spectacle cases, mending materials, letters and envelopes. There was also a Maling vase sporting a pattern of shiny pink scallops. The vase usually had faded artificial tulips in it. They played the game on a folding card table, covered with balding patches of green felt.

This particular Thursday, Edith Hill greeted her - 'Someone's moving into the flat upstairs! Mrs Barnett told me.'

And Freddy Hill, leading her to the paper-strewn settee, said, 'Yes - and the Warden thinks she's an artist! That's what she told Edith, anyway.'

Next morning, Sofie Stone called on Mrs Joelson to see if the old lady wanted any shopping. Although she'd just come down one floor in the lift and the corridors were cleaned daily, Sofie Stone felt she should be taking her shoes off at the old lady's door. Mrs Joelson was ninety-something and fond of conveying to her house - neighbours that she refused to live with her family because they were Kosher and untidy - two conditions she had no patience with. She paid a firm called 'Lilies' to clean and cook for her in Golda Meir House. She used a magnifying glass to identify coins where other old people just said, 'Here, take it out of my purse yourself.' Today she wanted peppermint creams in milk chocolate. MILK chocolate.

'Someone's moving into the empty flat on Monday,' Sofie Stone shouted.

'Who?'

'I don't know.'

'What?'

'An artist.'

What did it matter? They'd soon know. Or not.

After a moment Mrs Joelson commented, 'They're getting younger.'

No one knew what Sofie Stone's age was. Sometimes another resident would say in a guarded way, 'You moved here quite young, didn't you, Mrs Stone?'

Or even directly - 'So, how old are you, Sofie?'

But she just said, 'Go on then, guess. How old d'you think I am?'

And one person said sixty-eight, another seventy-six, another seventy. And Sofie Stone said, 'Very close,' to all of them.

On Monday a new name appeared on the Lobby Notice Board.

Miss Ruth Almond. Flat 18. 3rd Flr.

Flat 18 was next to one of the Communal Lounges and this was where Sofie met Miss Almond two evenings later. Miss

Almond's new T.V. set had not yet been delivered and on Sofie's set it was snowing on every channel. They both wanted to see a programme about antiques.

'Have you been a collector yourself?' Sofie asked, when it finished.

'I inherited some china,' Miss Almond replied. 'I added a few pieces over the years. It became quite valuable, actually. Now - well, I've no family, you know - so I sold it. There's no space here.'

Sofie knew. But you couldn't let everything go.

'All of it?'

'I kept a little floral dish - just the one. I specially liked it.'

'Yes. I collected coloured glass. I just kept one piece as well - for old time's sake. You know - a souvenir.'

'Like something from a holiday,' Miss Almond said, 'A souvenir from life.'

They both laughed.

'Yes,' Sofie agreed, 'A souvenir from a life.'

Miss Almond had a straight back and short, manicured white hair. She seemed able to see and walk well. She didn't cough. There weren't any obvious physical reasons why she should have given up her home. But Sofie knew that people's reasons were often not visible and sometimes very complicated.

Shortly afterwards, they met by chance in the lift. Ruth Almond said, 'How nice to see you again!'

When they reached the first floor and Sofie was about to step out, Ruth Almond stopped the lift door from closing and said, 'There's an Antiques Fayre at the Holiday Inn all weekend. Would you like to see the leaflet?'

And Sofie gave her flat number - number 7 on the first floor - and Ruth Almond said she'd bring the leaflet down when she'd had a rest and Sofie said, 'Oh, good heavens, yes.

I always need a rest in the afternoon!'

They had tea together in Sofie's sitting room and Ruth Almond admired the cut-glass bowl on the bedside table.

'What a lovely green,' she said, 'Light olive. Your candle's nearly used up, though.'

They arranged to go to the Antiques Fayre together and Sofie would order a taxi. Ruth Almond agreed to go on Saturday rather than Sunday.

'Sunday mornings aren't very convenient for me, ' Sofie said.

Saturday evening, after the outing, she clean forgot to replace the night-light by her bed, but she knew it would still burn in a small, transparent pool at the bottom of the bowl.

She didn't sleep well, her back and hips protesting at three hours of standing and shuffling at the Antiques Fayre. They'd stopped for a sandwich in a new 'Coffee Shop' at the hotel but the seats were metal and not cushioned.

'Post-Modern,' Ruth Almond had suggested.

In the morning, she woke up tired and pushed herself to the side of the bed. She lit the remains of the night-light and edged back under the warm duvet. She lay still on her back and thought about the exhibits, particularly the glass. Nothing as charming as her green bowl, though. She reviewed some of the old paintings they'd seen. There were so many! And real antiques, not like a Flea Market. If she'd had pots of money, she might have bought a little watercolour of daisies after rain, open where the sky had cleared, closed in the shade. Ruth Almond had talked about the pictures as they walked round. She explained she'd worked in an art gallery.

'It is a lovely little watercolour,' she'd said of the daisies, 'Would you buy it?'

'What? Now? In G. Meir House?'

'You're not dead yet,' Ruth Almond said.

During the week, Sofie played Scrabble with Edith and Freddy Hill and went shopping for Mrs Joelson, who wanted half a pound of Rum Fudge, NO raisins. She wrote to her younger son who lived in Vancouver and telephoned her older son who lived in Northern Ireland. She phoned him every week and would visit him again soon. She made coq au vin with dry sherry and ready-cut chicken pieces, and invited Ruth Almond to eat with her. She moved her old radio and made the dining table look as festive as she could. Ruth Almond arrived with a trifle from the supermarket and after they'd eaten they went up to her flat to watch the antiques programme, because her T.V. had been delivered now, but on Sofie's it was still snowing.

'Do you like coach outings?' Ruth Almond asked later. 'I used to go a lot at this time of year - the gardens are wonderful. Not quite Sissinghurst but there's usually a guided tour. And tea. And a stop for lunch.'

Sofie was uncertain. She didn't usually go on coach outings.

'I used to go with a friend,' Ruth Almond volunteered.

Sofie waited.

'She died. I couldn't bear to go last year. I could go again, I think. She'd like me to do that. It's nicer with someone else.'

'Why not?' Sophie said, 'Yes, why not.'

'It's on Sunday. Can you manage that? Sunday?'

They had to leave Golda Meir House early to be in the town centre for nine o'clock. The driver wore a smart blue blazer and helped Sofie up the three steps into the coach.

'That's a good idea,' he said, when he saw her stick.

Ruth showed her how to fasten her seat belt and asked at intervals if she was comfortable. Sofie talked about her proposed trip to Ireland. Ruth talked about gardens she'd visited. When Sophie asked about the friend who'd died,

Ruth said they'd known each other a long time.

It was a good day and Sofie readily agreed to go on the next Gardeners' Delight trip in two weeks' time.

The following Sunday she woke up later than usual and straightaway noticed how thirsty she felt. Then she remembered she'd introduced Ruth to Edith and Freddy the night before and Freddy had opened a bottle of wine.

She didn't usually drink wine.

She shuffled to the edge of the bed and got up. She slid her feet into her slippers and went into the kitchen. She made tea in her china mug with a tea bag and then set off across the big room back to her bed again.

Beside the radio, on the round dining table, was her olive green, cut glass Bohemian bowl and there was a new night-light in it.

'When did I do that?' she wondered.

She got back into bed with her tea, leaving the green bowl where it was.

DEAF, OR WHAT?
by Betty Weiner

'Who is he, Tom?'

'Dunno. Dick put him off the eleven o'clock.'

'Dick put him off? Is he a tramp? He looks like a tramp to me.'

Did they think he was deaf, or what? He got off to change trains and they grabbed him. Just as he was picking his bag up. Practically broke his arm, the porter feller. And pulling at his clothes. Next minute, a policeman's there and they're yakkety yakking over his head and the policeman's got his walkie-talkie out and they're pinning him together like he's a murderer or something.

'We'll just wait here for a moment, Sir.'

Breaking his arms and calling him 'Sir.' But when he tried to pick his bag up again the Policeman snapped,

'Just leave it where it is.'

Then the Station master arrived.

'We'll have a word in my office,' he said, 'What's your name?'

So he told them, 'William Pitt.'

He could manage a couple of steps, but not a staircase, not a railway bridge. There were two steps into his flats, but there was a ramp as well. Every time she saw him go out the Warden shouted, 'Use the ramp, Billy!'

They were dragging him up as though he'd refused to go with them. 'You can't sit down here,' the policeman said, when he missed his footing, pulling him up by his arm, wrecking his shoulder.

'Can't get up steps,' he got out.

'What?'

'What did he say?'

It was busy and noisy. People were looking at him, looking at them all. Giving them some distance but looking as they passed on the steps.

'Steps,' he said, when he caught his breath again, 'I can't get up them.'

They stopped. The porter feller looked like he didn't know what to do. The policeman said,

'Right. We'll soon see. Take him to the Sub's office, Tom.'

So they took him to an office on the same platform, the porter feller holding his arm, the policeman pulling at his wrist like a handcuff.

He could have gone across in the lift. He knew there was a lift, because the Warden had found out for him. Now he'd been sat in this office for an hour. And used like a criminal. Good job he hadn't told Geordie what time he was coming. What he really wanted was a drink.

'I hate tramps. There's no need for it, not these days.'

He recognised the policeman's voice outside the office.

'I'll phone Dick, find out what happened. Catch him before Peterborough. What about him?'

The other one said 'The Boss said let him know when we've got to the bottom of it. I'll keep an eye on him.'

They meant him. Did they think he was deaf or something?

He was sitting on an old wooden chair. His Tesco carrier bag had been dumped on a big square table beside him. It looked like a Sally Army table.

The one keeping an eye on him, the porter feller, looked in through the door.

'I'll just be outside. You're to wait here.'

William lifted his hand to try and stop him leaving.

'Can you gerrus a cuppa tea?'

'Where are you , Dick?'

'I'm in the cabin.'

'Boss wants to know what happened. This tramp you put off - -?

'I didn't put anyone off.'

'We've got him in the office - scruffy old man. Five three about. Skinny. Scotch jacket, black slip-ons. Grey hair all stuck together.'

'Tartan jacket without any elbows?'

'That's him, Dick.'

'I didn't put him off. He got off.'

'I thought you put him off.'

'No. I helped him. He's got a ticket for Chester. Asked me about platforms. I told him what to do - '

'He's got a ticket? What's he use for money?'

'Yeah, he's got a ticket. Didn't he show it to you?'

'He looks like a tramp.'

'I've seen worse'

'He smells.'

'He's got a ticket.'

'So why did you put him off?'

'I didn't put him off, Harry. I helped him.'

'So why have we got him, then?'

'Ask Tom. Tom was with him when we pulled out.'

In Chestnut House Mrs Springfield sat sideways with her feet on the pulled-out bottom drawer of her office desk. She'd kicked her black court shoes off and wondered vaguely when she'd have time to do her toe-nails again. She held a biro in her right hand and a mug of tea in her left, her elbow resting on a newspaper just where Margaret Thatcher's face was. Her Day Book was open in front of her and she was thinking about Billy Pitt, who had taken it into his head to travel across the country to visit a friend who was called George and lived in Chester. Billy could hardly breathe and he walked like a rickets relic. His flat was a tip and she had to bully him to have his clothes washed. She tried to persuade him to go to Chester by coach, but he said it took too long, and he was as stubborn as an old billy goat. At the end of the day, it was his own business what he did. She'd made enquiries about trains and booked the taxi and found out about station lifts. She'd done her best. She was accountable for what she could do, not what she couldn't do. Supposing she'd tried to stop him going? That would have been all over the papers. The Chronicle, then The Mirror and The Mail. Local Council Denies Resident his Rights. Housing Warden Behaves like Gaoler.

She pulled a face, thinking about his clothes. He'd gone with a clean set of underwear and she'd found him a pair of pyjamas. But he had difficulty dressing and he'd given up shirts with buttons. He wore vests and tee shirts and baggy jumpers, spotted with Meals on Wheels. He couldn't deal with trouser zips, so he left them undone and held his pants up with a canvas belt.

He needed something with elastic round the waist and she'd promised to look in a catalogue. You couldn't get anything in the shops. Poor sod, she thought, with his clumsy joints and wasted lungs. Why shouldn't he visit his friend?

Good luck to him!

She pushed the bottom drawer in with her foot and wrote in her Day Book: William Pitt got taxi to Central Station. Visiting friend in Chester. Back Saturday. Agreed clean room.

He was parched. You could die of thirst here. Mrs S told him to get a drink on the train, but he wasn't going to spend 50p on a tea bag. He shuffled across the room and looked out. He could see a lad outside, wearing station clothes. The lad looked at him the way strangers usually did, as though he was a mangy old cat. He beckoned him over.

'Gerrus some tea, will you, lad.'

'What you doing here?' the lad asked.

'Waiting. But I'm parched.'

The lad was going to walk away.

'Not well.'

'O.K. It's 65p.'

He was going to say, Stuff it, then, but his mouth was peeling. He pulled a coin out of his pocket and it fell on the floor. The lad picked it up and went to get tea. He made his way back to his chair in the office. The chair had lost most of its paint and reminded him of things. Waiting. All different kinds of waiting. Waiting and not knowing and gagging for a drink.

There'd been some mistake on the platform. Everything was all right until then. He got off the train, talked to the guard, tried to pick his bag up and they were all over him, breaking his arms, tearing at his clothes. Police. The lot. Crazy people.

'In here a minute, Tom.'

'Yes, Sir.'

'The old man on Platform One. You picked him up. Who is he?'

'I don't know - '

'Harry says Dick put him on the platform. Why have we got him?'

'I tried to help him, but he wouldn't let me.'

'Right. Go on, then, what happened?'

'He was flashing on the platform, Sir.'

'Flashing?'

'Not just his flies open - '

'He must be near eighty.'

'He had his trousers round his knees. He was just standing there with his pants down - looking round - showing himself. I tried to help him with his pants, but he hit me - pushed me off.'

'He dropped his pants?'

'They were round his legs - '

What about his underpants?'

'Didn't see any, Sir.'

'So what did you do?'

'I rushed over and tried to pull his pants up, and he started punching me and he lost his balance - '

'You knocked him over?'

'He fell on his bag. Well, he lost his balance, but I had a hold of him all the time. I called for assistance and Harry came running over. We got his pants up and called you.'

'Did he want the Gents? Who's talked to him so far?'

'Harry tried, but he couldn't get much out of him. He's on

his way to Chester.'

'So I gather. It says so on his ticket. Get Harry for me, will you.'

'Who is he, Harry?'

'Says he's called William Pitt.'

'Yes, I've got that.'

'On his way to Chester. Ten o'clock from Newcastle Central, changing -'

'Yes, changing here. Did you ask him about dropping his pants?'

'I could see he was going to give me some cock and bull story, they always do. You could fill a book with the excuses.

'What did he say, Harry?'

'I'd burn his clothes. Put him in fatigues. Lock him up for a few hours -'

'What, Harry?'

'I wrote it down. Took a while. Couldn't get anything out of him at first. He's got asthma or something.'

'So what did he say?'

'Not much. He said, "Eff off, Screw."'

About time, too, he thought, as the Station Master sat down opposite him at the Sally Army table. He'd had one cup of tea and no dinner. The sandwich Mrs S put in the top of his bag wasn't there any more. Probably fell out on the platform when they knocked him over. The Station Master was asking questions. These people always asked a lot of questions.

'My sandwich's gone,' he said.

'You're lucky you weren't arrested, Mr Pitt.'

Arrested? What for? The Station master was waiting for him to explain himself. He recognised the feel of it in the air - someone waiting for an explanation. Well, William, what have you got to say for yourself this time?

'Illegal to go on the York train - ' he got out in one breath and then, after another ' - is it?'

'You're lucky you weren't arrested for exposing yourself in public.'

'What?'

'Dropping your pants on Platform 1,' the Station Master said. 'I'd have thought you'd be past that by now.'

The man must be an idiot. People in uniforms usually were. He stared at the Station Master and said nothing.

'You've got a return ticket for Chester. You came in on the London train and got off here for the Liverpool train. My staff find you on Platform 1 with your pants down and making no effort to cover yourself up. It's an offence, you know.'

Bugger off, he thought. What do you know about anything?

'Fell down,' he offered, after a few moments. The Station Master looked as though he didn't understand. 'Slipped off. Lousy belt.'

He pointed to his canvas belt. One of the station lads had tied it up again for him.

'Your zip's open now!'

He didn't answer. Let the man work it out for himself.

Then there were questions about where he was going, who he was going to see, where he lived, the name of the Warden. Did he have the telephone number? He pointed to the Tesco bag and the other man emptied the contents onto the table. Pyjamas, underpants, tee-shirt, squashed up plastic mac. An envelope with the Chestnut House number. Mrs S had put it on the back of his letter from George. The letter said, 'See you wed scout keep out of trouble ha ha. Geordie.'

The Station Master read the letter and put it back with the clothes. He kept the envelope.

'Wait here,' he said.

Wait here. He'd like a pound for every time he'd been told to wait here.

'Can you gerrus a sandwich?' he asked. And when the Station master turned back to look at him he said, 'Get my dinner at twelve - delivered.'

Mrs Springfield was eating a pork and pease-pudding stottie in her office at half past one when the phone rang. She let it ring, while she chewed and swallowed and took a mouthful of tea. The caller announced himself as the Station Master at York Railway Station. She'd never had a Station Master on the line before. Sometimes she had to deal with arrogant relatives, often she had doctors on the phone, councillors, too, from time to time. But never a Station Master up till now. It was like collecting scalps and she enjoyed it.

She managed not to laugh at the idea of Billy Pitt flashing on Platform 1. She'd told him often enough if his pants fell off he'd be locked up for being a pervert. She explained to the Station Master that Mr Pitt had a problem with fine motor skills. He couldn't do buttons and zips. His belt had probably come loose. He didn't have much breath so it would take him time to get himself organised. Yes, he was stubborn. Stubborn, old and harmless. He wanted to visit a friend in Chester. She thought they'd probably been on the road together. Or at sea. She wasn't sure.

The Station Master said they were going to send him back. Mrs Springfield said that didn't make any sense. Billy had been looking forward to going and his friend was expecting him. He wasn't stupid or confused and he had a right to go.

The Station Master said he was putting him on the 2.30 back to Newcastle. The Guard would keep an eye on him and put him off at Central Station. Would she like to pick him up from there? She said no, she wouldn't. He said no matter, the Railway Police would collect him off the train and make sure he got back safely. He wasn't fit to be out.

Mrs Springfield said he went out all the time and why couldn't he just go on to Chester as planned? The Station Master said he wasn't fit to be travelling alone and they could take no responsibility for him except to get him home as quickly as possible.

'Nobody wants you to take responsibility! Just make sure his belt's fastened and send him on his way.'

'I'm putting him on the 2.30 home again.'

'What about his friend? He's expected in Chester.'

'I can't help that. Can you let him know?'

She saw that his mind was made up.

'I'll see what I can do,' and she slammed the phone down.

She glanced at her tea and snorted. She picked up the pork bun, held it in her hand for a moment then threw it in the waste bin.

'Oh, shit,' she said out loud.

'Use the ramp, Billy!'

It was nice to hear a familiar voice. It was nice to hear Mrs S telling him to use the ramp like she always did. Like he always did, anyway. Though he'd move towards the steps sometimes to keep her on her toes. Use the ramp, Billy. He hadn't realised how much this flat felt like home. He thought it was just a room. Like other places had been just rooms. Or bunks. This felt like when he had a home with a woman in it.

'I see you've been brought back in style,' Mrs S said, as the Police car turned round outside Chestnut House. She was holding the door open for him, not expecting him to rush.

'Didn't work out then,' she said.

He stopped inside to get his breath back. Mrs S walked along the corridor with him to his room.

'Your flat's nice and tidy. Good job it was done straight

away.'

'I'm not paying,' he said.

He dropped his Tesco bag on the floor and sank into his armchair. He was tired and he couldn't be bothered. It was what women always wanted to do - move things about and wash clothes.

'Filled a bin bag, nearly, with rubbish off your floors. Cartons and wrappers and chip papers. What're you like, Billy Pitt!'

He opened his eyes.

'What about those pants?'

'I've sent away for them.'

'What about Geordie?' he asked.

'I phoned. The shop next door. You gave me the number, remember?'

'I'll drop him a note.'

He said nothing for another minute, sat with his eyes closed, knew she was still there. Making sure he was alright.

'Will you gerrus some paper?'

'He'll think it's Christmas,' she said.

Later, she brought him a piece of writing paper with 'Chestnut House' stamped on the top. It looked like it had been done with little rubber blocks. He'd had one of those as a lad: John Bull Printing Set. He'd 'printed' letters for all his friends, put bits of paper through all their letter-boxes.

He wrote to Geordie with a cracked biro, telling him some officious bastard had sent him home from York. When he got his money back off them, he'd travel again.

Mrs Springfield sorted out the post and decided to take the letter addressed to 'Mister Bill Pit' to him in his room. She knew who it was from. She waited while he opened it, watched his face. At first there was no reaction. She could see it was a short message and he was reading it over again. Then he passed it to her to read. She looked over the top of the sheet at him and he was smiling now, at least his eyes were. The letter said, 'Come on the coach, ye daft bugger - Geordie.'

Biographies

Linda Leatherbarrow
is three times 1st Prize Winner of the London Writers competition. In 2001 she won a Bridport Prize for her story 'Ride' and an Asham Award. Her stories have been published in magazines including Ambit, Cosmopolitan and Writing Women and in the anthologies Harlot Red, The Nerve, Signals 2, Sleeping Rough and The British Council's New Writing 8. They have also been broadcast on BBC Radio 4.

Mary Lowe
was born in Bath in 1959 but moved to London when she was four to seek her fortune. She has done a variety of jobs including teaching, training, health promotion and youth work. Since 1984 she's been living in Newcastle with partner Maggie and two computers (one for each hand). She is currently writing a novel with her left hand and a musical with her right. She's involved in the organisation of Proudwords, the UK's only creative writing festival for lesbians, gay men and bisexuals. Her stories have appeared in various anthologies including New Welsh Review, Long Journey Home (Women's Press), City Secrets (Commonword) and Fruits of Labour (Women's Press)

Janine Langley McCann
grew up in Pudsey, Leeds, but has lived in Newcastle almost ten years now. She is 42, has 2 children, a son of 26 and a daughter of 7. Though she has attended various business training courses in the past, her first ever educational qualification, achieved in 2001, was an MA (in Creative Writing of course). She has now abandoned herself to her

creative side and when she's not writing she's teaching Creative Writing and Key Skills to Performing Arts and other FE students.

Janine's short stories have previously been published in several literary journals and she is hoping soon to complete her first novel.

She would like to dedicate her work here to her lovely Dad Jim, who she lost earlier this year.

Susannah Rickards

Before writing, Susannah was an actress. Then she realised everything good about acting: living vicarious lives, researching other worlds, entering different states of mind, was demanded even more by writing, and she didn't have to hang around to get someone to ask her to do it, or wear make up that brought her out in blotches. As a writer she can play an African man or a pubescent boy, and do it, she hopes, with some authenticity. She doesn't even miss out on the boozing, bitching and whinging - writers do that too.

Betty Weiner

Betty Weiner was born in Vienna in 1936 very shortly after her twin brother. When she was 2 years old, her parents were given notice to quit their municipal apartment and her father informed that his dental services were no longer required in Austria. An official letter bearing a swastika informed them they could leave. Using an Underground organisation they entered Belgium as illegal immigrants and, after 6 months in hiding in Brussels, gained visas for England.

Betty grew up in North Wales. First in Mold, a small market town, and later in Prestatyn, by the sea. She attended Mold Board School, Rhyl Grammar School and then Birmingham University, where she met her husband. His family were refugees from Prague. She spent two years teaching Juniors, some years having babies and doing voluntary work and then qualified as a Social Worker. She spent about twenty years working in North Tyneside and Newcastle with families in stress and with all kinds of children with problems - offending children, orphaned children, disturbed and abused children.

Since retirement she's got on with her writing 'career', and attended literature and writing classes, and writers' workshops.

Especially significant for prose writing have been northern tutors Celia Bryce, Margaret Wilkinson and Michael Ayton. And for encouragement, too, Ellen Phethean of Diamond Twig. She's had pieces in Northern New Writers, Northern Tales, The Blue Room Anthology, Mslexia magazine and Radio 4's short story slot.

The two stories which are included in this anthology came out of visits to Sheltered Housing, one block in Coxlodge, Newcastle, the other in Crouch End, North London.